JOHN T. SLADEK was

England. He was educ
where he studied mecha
ture. Since then he has
draughtsman, and a rai
ductive System was publ
his humorous style of writing has been likened to the work of Vonnegut.

Also by John Sladek

The Steam-driven Boy
The Müller-Fokker Effect
Black Alice
The Reproductive System
The New Apocrypha

John Sladek

Keep the Giraffe Burning

PANTHER
GRANADA PUBLISHING
London Toronto Sydney New York

Published by Granada Publishing Limited
in Panther Books 1977

ISBN 0 586 04757 3

A Panther Original

Granada Publishing Limited
Frogmore, St Albans, Herts AL2 2NF
and
3 Upper James Street, London W1R 4BP
1221 Avenue of the Americas, New York, NY 10020, USA
117 York Street, Sydney, NSW 2000 Australia
100 Skyway Avenue, Toronto, Ontario, Canada M9W 3A6
Trio City, Coventry Street, Johannesburg 2001, South Africa
CML Centre, Queen & Wyndham, Auckland 1, New Zealand

Made and printed in Great Britain by
Cox & Wyman Ltd, London, Reading and Fakenham

Contents

Foreword

Don't be fooled by the Surrealist title. Most of these stories are only meant to be fun, and no serious messages are intended.

Surrealism is supposed to have something to do with Freud and dreams, which doesn't sound entertaining at all. Psychiatrists know how boring re-told dreams can be, and so do the husbands and wives of dreamers, at their breakfast tables. Freud never strikes you as exactly a barrel of fun either, does he? Especially after he came down from Mount Ararat with the graven tables of Dream Interpretation.

Probably what was wrong with Surrealism all along was that it got defined precisely and interpreted exactly. Nothing can stand up to that. Think of all the serious critics who've gone over and over *The Castle of Otranto*, until it's lost most of its original appeal. I've met dozens of people who've read this gothic classic through without laughing.

Readers who don't like laughing can have their own kind of entertainment out of this collection. If they will only frown and bear it, reading all of the stories, they will find an exact interpretation in the Afterword. A friend of mine wrote it, and I believe it spoils every story here.

People have laughed at all great inventors and discoverers. They laughed at Galileo, at Edison's light bulb, and even at nitrous oxide. I hope they will laugh, a little, at these stories.

Elephant with Wooden Leg

Note: Madmen are often unable to distinguish between dream, reality, and ... between dream and reality. None of the incidents in Henry LaFarge's narrative ever happened or could have happened. His 'Orinoco Institute' bears no relation to the actual think tank of that name, his 'Drew Blenheim' in no way resembles the famous futurologist, and his 'United States of America' is not even a burlesque upon the real United States of Armorica.

I couldn't hear him.

'Can't hear you, Blenheim. The line must be bad.'

'Or mad, Hank. I wonder what that would take?'

'What what?'

'What would it take to drive a telephone system out of its mind, eh? So that it wasn't just giving wrong numbers, but madly right ones. Let's see: Content-addressable computer memories to shift the conversations ...'

I stopped listening. A bug was crawling up the window frame across the room. It moved like a cockroach, but I couldn't be sure.

'Look, Blenheim, I'm pretty busy today. Is there something on your mind?'

He ploughed right on. '... so if you're trying to reserve a seat on the plane to Seville, you'd get a seat at the opera instead. While the person who wants the opera seat is really making an appointment with a barber, whose customer is just then talking to the box-office of *Hair*, or maybe making a hairline reservation ...'

'Blenheim, I'm talking to you.'

'Yes?'

'What was it you called me up about?'

'Oh, this and that. I was wondering, for instance, whether parrots have internal clocks.'

'What?' I still couldn't be sure whether the bug was a cockroach or not, but I saluted just in case.

'If so, maybe we could get them to act as speaking clocks.'

He sounded crazier than ever. What trivial projects for one of the best brains in our century – no wonder he was on leave.

'Blenheim, I'm busy. Institute work must go on, you know.'

'Yes. Tell you what, why don't you drop over this afternoon? I have something to talk over with you.'

'Can't. I have a meeting all afternoon.'

'Fine, fine. See you, then. Anytime around 4:43.'

Madmen never listen.

Helmut Rasmussen came in just as Blenheim hung up. He seemed distressed. Not that his face showed it; ever since that bomb wrecked his office, Hel has been unable to move his face. Hysterical paralysis, Dr Grobe had explained.

But Hel could signal whatever he felt by fiddling with the stuff in his shirt pocket. For anger, his red pencil came out (and sometimes underwent a savage sharpening), impatience made him work his slide rule, surprise made him glance into his pocket diary, and so on.

Just now he was clicking the button on his ballpoint pen with some agitation. For a moment he actually seemed about to take it out and draw worry lines on his forehead.

'What is it, Hel? The costing on Project Faith?' He spread the schedules on my desk and pointed to the snag: a discrepancy between the estimated cost of blasting apart and hauling away the Rocky Mountains, and the value of oil recovered in the process.

'I see. The trains, eh? Diesels seem to use most of the oil we get. How about steam locomotives, then?'

He clapped me on the shoulder and nodded.

'By the way, Hel, I won't be at the meeting today. Blenheim just called up. Wants to see me.'

Hel indicated surprise.

'Look, I know he's a crackpot. You don't have to pocket-diary me, I know he's nuts. But he is also technically still the Director. Our boss. They haven't taken him off the payroll, just put him on sick leave. Besides, he used to have a lot of good ideas.'

Hel took out a felt-tip pen and began to doodle with some sarcasm. The fact was, Blenheim had completely lost his grip during his last year at the Institute. Before the government forced him to take leave, he'd been spending half a million a year on developing, rumours said, glass pancakes. And who could forget his plan to arm police with chocolate revolvers?

'Sure he's had a bad time, but maybe he's better now,' I said, without conviction.

Institute people never get better, Hel seemed to retort. They just kept on making bigger and better decisions, with more and more brilliance and finality, until they broke. Like glass pancakes giving out an ever purer ring, they exploded.

It was true. Like everyone else here, I was seeing Dr Grobe, our resident psychiatrist, several times a week. Then there were cases beyond even the skill of Dr Grobe: Joe Feeney, who interrupted his work (on the uses of holograms) one day to announce that he was a filing cabinet. Edna Bessler, who believed that she was being pursued by a synthetic *a priori* proposition. The lovely entomologist Pawlie Sutton, who disappeared. And George Hoad, whose rocket research terminated when he walked into the Gents one day and cut his throat. George spent the last few minutes of consciousness vainly trying to mop up the bloody floor with toilet paper . . .

Something was wrong with the personnel around this place, all right. And I suspected that our little six-legged masters knew more about this than they were saying.

Finally I mumbled, 'I know it's useless, Hel. But I'd better find out what he wants.'

You do what you think is best, Hel thought. He stalked out of my office then, examining the point on his red pencil.

The bug was a cockroach, *P. americana.* It sauntered across the wall until it reached the curly edge of a wall poster, then it flew about a foot to land on the nearest dark spot. This was Uncle Sam's right eye. Uncle Sam, with his accusing eyes and finger, was trying to recruit men for the Senate and House of Representatives. On this poster, he said, 'The Senate Needs MEN'. So far, the recruitment campaign was a failure. Who could blame people for not wanting to go on the 'firing line' in Washington? The casualty rate of Congressmen was 30 per cent annually, and climbing, in spite of every security measure we could think of.

Which reminded me of work. I scrubbed off the blackboard and started laying out a contingency tree for Project Pogo, a plan to make the whole cabinet – all one hundred and forty-three secretaries – completely mobile, hence, proof against revolution. So far the Security Secretary didn't care for the idea of 'taking to our heels', but it was cheaper to keep the cabinet on the move than to guard them in Washington.

The cockroach, observing my industry, left by a wall ventilator, and I breathed easier. The contingency tree didn't look so interesting by now, and out the window I could see real trees.

The lawn rolled away down from the building to the river (not the Orinoco, despite our name). The far bank was blue-black with pines, and the three red maples on our lawn, this time of year, stood out like three separate, brilliant fireballs. For just the duration of a bluejay's flight from one to another, I could forget about the stale routine, the smell of chalkdust.

I remembered a silly day three years ago, when I'd carved a heart on one of those trees, with Pawlie Sutton's initials and my own.

Now a security guard strolled his puma into view. They stopped under the nearest maple and he snapped the animal's lead. It was up the trunk in two bounds, and out of sight among the leaves. While that stupid-faced man in uniform looked up, the fireball shook and swayed above him. A few great leaves fell, bright as drops of blood.

Now what was *this* headache going to be about?

All the big problems were solved, or at least we knew how to solve them. The world was just about the way we wanted it, now, except we no longer seemed to want it that way. That's how Mr Howell, the Secretary of Personal Relationships, had put it in his telecast. What was missing? God, I think he said. God had made it possible for us to dam the Amazon and move the Orinoco, to feed India and dig gold from the ocean floor and cure cancer. And now God – the way he said it made you feel that He, too, was in the Cabinet – God was going to help us get down and solve our personal, human problems. Man's inhumanity to man. The lack of communication. The hatred. God and Secretary Howell were going to get right down to some committee work on this. I think that was the telecast where Howell announced the introduction of detention camps for 'malcontents'. Just until we got our personal problems all ironed out. I had drawn up the plans for these camps that summer. Then George Hoad borrowed my pocket-knife one day and never gave it back. Then the headaches started.

As I stepped outside, the stupid-faced guard was looking up the skirt of another tree.

'Prrt, prrt,' he said quietly, and the black puma dropped to earth beside him. There was something hanging out of its mouth that looked like a bluejay's wing.

'Good girl. Good girl.'

I hurried away to the helicopter.

Drew Blenheim's tumbledown mansion sits in the middle of withered woods. For half a mile around, the trees are laced together with high-voltage fence. Visitors are blindfolded and brought in by helicopter. There are also rumours of minefields and other security measures. At that time, I put it all down to Blenheim's paranoia.

The engine shut down with the sound of a coin spinning to

rest. Hands helped me out and removed my blindfold. The first thing I saw, hanging on a nearby stretch of fence, was a lump of bones and burnt fur from some small animal. The guards and their submachine-guns escorted me only as far as the door, for Blenheim evidently hated seeing signs of the security he craved. The house looked dismal and decayed – the skull of some dead Orinoco Institute?

A servant wearing burnt cork makeup and white gloves ushered me through a dim hallway that smelled of hay and on into the library.

'I'll tell Mr Blenheim you're here, sir. Perhaps you'd care to read one of his monographs while you wait?'

I flicked through *The Garden of Regularity* (a slight tract recommending that older people preserve intestinal health by devouring their own dentures) and opened an insanely boring book called *Can Bacteria Read?* I was staring uncomprehendingly at one of its pages when a voice said:

'Are you still here?' The plump old woman had evidently been sitting in her deep chair when I came in. As she craned around at me, I saw she had a black eye. Something was wrong with her hair, too. 'I thought you'd left by now – oh, it's *you*.'

'Madam, do I know you?'

She sat forward and put her face to the light. The black eye was tattooed, and the marcelled hair was really a cap of paper, covered with wavy ink lines. But it was Edna Bessler, terribly aged.

'You've changed, Edna.'

'So would you, young man, if you'd been chased around a nuthouse for two years by a synthetic *a priori* proposition.' She sniffed. 'Well, thank heavens the revolution is set for tomorrow.'

I laughed nervously. 'Well, Edna, it certainly is good to see you. What are you doing here, anyway?'

'There are quite a few of the old gang here, Joe Feeney and – and others. This place has become a kind of repair depot for mad futurologists. Blenheim is very kind, but of course he's quite mad himself. Mad as a wet hen. As you see from his writing.'

'*Can Bacteria Read?* I couldn't read it.'

'Oh, he thinks that germs are, like people, amenable to suggestion. So, with the proper application of mass hypnosis among the microbe populations, we ought to be able to cure any illness with any quack remedy.'

I nodded. 'Hope he recovers soon. I'd like to see him back at the Institute, working on real projects again. Big stuff, like the old days. I'll never forget the old Drew Blenheim, the man who invented satellite dialling.'

Satellite dialling came about when the malcontents were trying to jam government communications systems, cut lines and blow up exchanges. Blenheim's system virtually made each telephone a complete exchange in itself, dialling directly through a satellite. Voice signals were compressed and burped skywards in short bursts that evaded most jamming signals. It was an Orinoco Institute triumph over anarchy.

Edna chuckled. 'Oh, he's working on real projects. I said he was mad, not useless. Now if you'll help me out of this chair, I must go fix an elephant.'

I was sure I'd misheard this last. After she'd gone, I looked over a curious apparatus in the corner. Parts of it were recognizable – a clock inside a parrot cage, a gas laser, and a fringed shawl suspended like a flag from a walking-stick thrust into a watermelon – but their combination was baffling.

At 4:43 by the clock in the cage, the blackface servant took me to a gloomy great hall place, scattered with the shapes of easy chairs and sofas. A figure in a diving suit rose from the piano and waved me to a chair. Then it sat down again, flipping out its airhoses behind the bench.

For a few minutes I suffered through a fumbling version of some Mexican tune. But when Blenheim – no doubt it was he – stood up and started juggling oranges, I felt it was time to speak out.

'Look, I've interrupted my work to come here. Is this all you have to show me?'

One of the oranges vaulted high, out of sight in the gloom above; another hit me in the chest. The figure opened its face-plate and grinned. 'Long time no see, Hank.'

It was me.

'Rubber mask,' Blenheim explained, plucking at it. 'I couldn't resist trying it on you, life gets so tedious here. Ring for Rastus, will you? I want to shed this suit.'

We made small talk while the servant helped him out of the heavy diving suit. Rather, Blenheim rattled on alone; I wasn't feeling well at all. The shock of seeing myself had reminded me of something I should remember, but couldn't.

'. . . to build a heraldry vending machine. Put in a coin, punch out your name, and it prints a coat-of-arms. Should suit those malcontents, eh? All they probably really want is a coat-of-arms.'

'They're just plain evil,' I said. 'When I think how they bombed poor Hel Rasmussen's office—'

'Oh, he did that himself. Didn't you know?'

'Suicide? So that explains the hysterical paralysis!'

My face looked exasperated, as Blenheim peeled it off. 'Is that what Dr Grobe told you? Paralysed hell, the blast blew his face clean off. Poor Hel's present face is a solid plate of plastic, bolted on. He breathes through a hole in his shoulder and feeds himself at the armpit. If Grobe told you any different, he's just working on your morale.'

From upstairs came a kind of machine-gun clatter. The minstrel servant glided in with a tray of drinks.

'Oh, Rastus. Tell the twins not to practise their tap-dancing just now, will you? Hank looks as if he has a headache.'

'Yes sir. By the way, the three-legged elephant has arrived. I put it in the front hall. I'm afraid the prosthesis doesn't fit.'

'I'll fix it. Just ask Jumbo to lean up against the wall for half an hour.'

'Very good, sir.'

After this, I decided to make my escape from this Bedlam.

'Doesn't anybody around here ever do anything straightforward or say anything in plain English?'

'We're trying to tell you something, Hank, but it isn't easy. For one thing, I'm not sure we can trust you.'

'Trust me for what?'

His twisted face twisted out a smile. 'If you don't know, then how can we trust you? But come with me to the conservatory and I'll show you something.'

We went to a large room with dirty glass walls. To me it looked like nothing so much as a bombed-out workshop. Though there were bags of fertilizer on the floor, there wasn't a living plant in sight. Instead, the tables were littered with machinery and lab equipment: jumbles of retorts and coloured wires and nuts and bolts that made no sense.

'What do you see, Hank?'

'Madness and chaos. You might as well have pears in the light sockets and a banana on the telephone cradle, for all I can make of it.'

He laughed. 'That's better. We'll crazify you yet.'

I pointed to a poster-covered cylinder standing in the corner. One of the posters had Uncle Sam, saying 'I Need MEN for Congress'.

'What's that Parisian advertising kiosk doing here?'

'Rastus built that for us, out of scrap alloys I had lying around. Like it?'

I shrugged. 'The top's too pointed. It looks like—'

'Yes, go on.'

'This is silly. All of you need a few sessions with Dr Grobe,' I said. 'I'm leaving.'

'I was afraid you'd say that. But it's you who need another session with Dr Grobe, Hank.'

'You think *I'm* crazy?'

'No, you're too damned sane.'

'Well you sure as hell are nuts!' I shouted. 'Why bother with all the security outside? Afraid someone will steal the idea of a minstrel show or the secret of a kiosk?'

He laughed again. 'Hank, those guards aren't there to keep

strangers out. *They're to keep us in.* You see, my house really and truly is a madhouse.'

I stamped out a side door and ordered my helicopter.

'My head's killing me,' I told the guard. 'Take it easy with that blindfold.'

'Oh, sorry, mac. Hey look, it's none of my business, but what did you do with that tree you brung with you?'

'Tree?' God, even the guards were catching it.

That evening I went to see Dr Grobe.

'Another patient? I swear, I'm going to install a revolving door on this office. Sit down. Uh, Hank LaFarge, isn't it? Sit down, Hank. Let's see . . . oh, you're the guy who's afraid of cockroaches, right?'

'Not exactly afraid of them. In fact they remind me of someone I used to be fond of. Pawlie Sutton used to work with them. But my problem is, I know that cockroaches are the real bosses. We're just kidding ourselves with our puppet government, our Uncle Sham—'

He chuckled appreciatively.

'But what "bugs" me is, nobody will recognize this plain and simple truth, Doctor.'

'Ah, ah. Remember last time, you agreed to call me by my first name.'

'Sorry, uh, Oddpork.' I couldn't imagine why anyone with that name wanted to be called by it, unless the doctor himself was trying to get used to it. He was an odd-pork of a man, too: plump and rumpy, with over-large hands that never stopped adjusting his already well-adjusted clothes. He always looked surprised at everything I said, even 'hello'. Every session, he made the same joke about the revolving door.

Still, repetitive jokes help build a family atmosphere, which was probably what he wanted. There was a certain comfort in this stale atmosphere of no surprises. Happy families are all alike, and their past is exactly like their future.

'Hank, I haven't asked you directly about your cockroach theory before, have I? Want to tell me about it?'

'I know it sounds crazy at first. For one thing, cockroaches aren't very smart, I know that. In some ways, they're stupider than ants. And their communication equipment isn't much, either. Touch and smell, mainly. They aren't naturally equipped for conquering the world.'

Oddpork lit a cigar and leaned back, looking at the ceiling. 'What do they do with the world when they get it?'

'That's another problem. After all, they don't *need* the world. All they need is food, water, a fair amount of darkness and some warmth. But there's the key, you see?

'I mean we humans have provided for all these needs for many centuries. Haphazardly, though. So it stands to reason that life would be better for them if we worked for them on a regular basis. But to get us to do that, they have to take over first.'

He tried to blow a smoke ring, failed, and adjusted his tie. 'Go on. How do they manage this takeover?'

'I'm not sure, but I think they have help. Maybe some smart tinkerer wanted to see what would happen if he gave them good long-distance vision. Maybe he was so pleased with the result that he then taught them to make semaphore signals with their feelers. The rest is history.'

Dusting his lapel, Dr Grobe said, 'I don't quite follow. Semaphore signals?'

'One cockroach is stupid. But a few thousand of them in good communication could make up a fair brain. Our tinkerer probably hastened that along by intensive breeding and group learning problems, killing off the failures . . . it would take ten years at the outside.'

'Really? And how long would the conquest of man take? How would the little insects fare against the armies of the world?'

'They never need to try. Armies are run by governments, and governments are run, for all practical purposes, by small panels of experts. Think tanks like the Orinoco Institute. And – this just occurred to me – for all practical purposes, you run the Institute.'

For once, Dr Grobe did not looked surprised. 'Oh, so I'm in on the plot, am I?'

'We're all so crazy, we really depend on you. You can ensure that we work for the good of the cockroaches, or else you can get rid of us – send us away, or encourage our suicides.'

'Why should I do that?'

'Because *you* are afraid of them.'

'Not at all.' But his hand twitched, and a little cigar ash fell on his immaculate trousers. I felt my point was proved.

'Damn. I'll have to sponge that. Excuse me.'

He stepped into his private washroom and closed the door. My feeling of triumph suddenly faded. Maybe I was finally cracking. What evidence did I really have?

On the other hand, Dr Grobe was taking a long time in there. I stole over to the washroom door and listened.

'. . . verge of suicide . . .,' he murmured. '. . . yes . . . give up the idea, but . . . yes, that's just what I . . .'

I threw back the door on a traditional spy scene. In the half-darkness, Dr G was hunched over the medicine cabinet, speaking into a microphone. He wore earphones.

'Hank, don't be a foo—'

I hit him, not hard, and he sat down on the edge of the tub. He looked resigned.

'So this is my imagined conspiracy, is it? Where do these wires lead?'

They led inside the medicine cabinet, to a tiny apparatus. A dozen brown ellipses had clustered around it, like a family around the TV.

'Let me explain,' he said.

'Explanations are unnecessary, Doctor. I just want to get out of here, unless your six-legged friends can stop me.'

'They might. So could I. I could order the guards to shoot you. I could have you put away with your crazy friends. I could even have you tried for murder, just now.'

'Murder?' I followed his gaze back into the office. From under the desk, a pair of feet. 'Who's that?'

'Hel Rasmussen. Poisoned himself a few minutes before you

came in. Believe me, it wasn't pleasant, seeing the poor fellow holding a bottle of cyanide to his armpit. He left a note blaming you, in a way.'

'Me!'

'You were the last straw. This afternoon, he saw you take an axe and deliberately cut down one of those beautiful maple trees in the yard. Destruction of beauty – it was too much for him.'

Trees again. I went to the office window and looked out at the floodlit landscape. One of the maples was missing.

Dr Grobe and I sat down again at our respective interview stations, while I thought this over. Blenheim and his mask came into it, I was sure of that. But why?

Dr Grobe fished his lifeless cigar from the ashtray. 'The point is, I can stop you from making any trouble for me. So you may as well hear me out.' He scratched a match on the sole of Hel's shoe and relit the cigar.

'All right, Oddpork. You win. What happens now?'

'Nothing much. Nothing at all. If my profession has any meaning, it's to keep things from happening.' He blew out the match. 'I'm selling ordinary life. Happiness, as you must now see, lies in developing a pleasant, comfortable and productive routine – and then sticking to it. No unpleasant surprises. No shocks. Psychiatry has always aimed for that, and now it is within our grasp. The cockroach conspiracy hasn't taken over the world, but it has taken over the Institute – and it's our salvation.

'You see, Hank, our bargain isn't one-sided. We give them a little shelter, a few scraps of food. But they give us something far more important: real organization. *The life of pure routine.*'

I snorted. 'Like hurrying after trains? Or wearing ourselves out on assembly-line work? Or maybe grinding our lives away in boring offices? Punching time-clocks and marching in formation?'

'None of the above, thank you. Cockroaches never hurry to anything but dinner. They wouldn't march in formation except for fun. They are free – yet they are part of a highly organized society. And this can be ours.'

'If we're not all put in detention camps.'

'Listen, those camps are only a stage. So what if a few million grumblers get sterilized and shut away for a year or two? Think of the *billions* of happy, decent citizens, enjoying a freedom they have earned. Someday, every man will live exactly as he pleases – and his pleasure will lie in serving his fellow men.'

Put like that, it was persuasive. Another half-hour of this and I was all but convinced.

'Sleep on it, eh Hank? Let me know tomorrow what you think.' His large hand on my shoulder guided me to the door.

'You may be right,' I said, smiling back at him. I meant it, too. Even though the last thing I saw, as the door closed, was a stream of glistening brown that came from under the washroom door and disappeared under the desk.

I sat up in my own office most of the night, staring out at the maple stump. There was no way out: Either I worked for *Periplaneta americana* and gradually turned into a kind of moral cockroach myself, or I was killed. And there were certain advantages to either choice.

I was about to turn on the video-recorder to leave a suicide note, when I noticed the cassette was already recorded. I ran it back and played it.

Blenheim came on, wearing my face and my usual suit.

'They think I'm you, Hank, dictating some notes. Right now you're really at my house, reading a dull book in the library. So dull, in fact, that it's guaranteed to put you into a light trance. When I'm safely back, Edna will come in and wake you.

'She's not as loony as she seems. The black eye is inked for her telescope, and the funny cap with lines on it, that looks like marcelled hair, that's a weathermap. I won't explain why she's doing astronomy – you'll understand in time.

'On the other hand, she's got a fixation that the stars are nothing but the shiny backs of cockroaches, treading around the heavenly spheres. It makes a kind of sense when you think of it: *Periplaneta* means around the world, and America being the home of the Star-Spangled Banner.

'Speaking of national anthems, Mexico's is La Cucaracha – another cockroach reference. They seem to be taking over this message!

'The gang and I have been thinking about bugs a lot lately. Of course Pawlie has always thought about them, but the rest of us . . .' I missed the next part. So Pawlie was at the madhouse? And they hadn't told me?

'. . . when I started work on the famous glass pancakes. I discovered a peculiar feature of glass discs, such as those found on clock faces.

'Say, you can do us a favour. I'm coming around at dawn with the gang, to show you a gadget or two. We haven't got all the bugs out of them yet, but – will you go into Dr Grobe's office at dawn, and check the time on his clock? But first, smash the glass on his window, will you? Thanks. I'll compensate him for it later.

'Then go outside the building, but on no account stand between the maple stump and the broken window. The best place to wait is on the little bluff to the North, where you'll have a good view of the demonstration. We'll meet you there.

'Right now you see our ideas darkly, as through a pancake, I guess. But soon you'll understand. You see, we're a kind of cockroach ourselves. I mean, living on scraps of sanity. We have to speak in parables and work in silly ways because *they* can't. *They* live in a comfortable kind of world where elephants have their feet cut off to make umbrella stands. We have to make good use of the three-legged elephants.

'Don't bother destroying this cassette. It won't mean a thing to any right-living insect.'

It didn't mean much to me, not yet. Cockroaches in the stars? Clocks? There were questions I had to ask, at the rendezvous.

There was one question I'd already asked that needed an

answer. Pawlie had been messing about in her lab, when I asked her to marry me. Two years ago, was it? Or three?

'But you don't like cockroaches,' she said.

'No, and I'll never ask a cockroach for its claw in marriage.' I looked over her shoulder into the glass case. 'What's so interesting about these?'

'Well, for one thing, they're not laboratory animals. I caught them myself in the basement here at the Institute. See? Those roundish ones are the nymphs – sexless adolescents. Cute, aren't they?'

I had to admit they were. A little. 'They look like the fat black exclamation points in comic strips,' I observed.

'They're certainly healthy, all of them. I've never seen any like them. I— that's funny.' She went and fetched a book, and looked from some illustration to the specimens under glass.

'What's funny?'

'Look, I'm going to be dissecting the rest of the afternoon. Meet you for dinner. Bye.'

'You haven't answered my question, Pawlie.'

'Bye.'

That was the last I saw of her. Later, Dr Grobe put it about that she'd been found, hopelessly insane. Still later, George Hoad cut his throat.

The floodlights went off, and I could see dawn greyness and mist. I took a can of beans and went for a stroll outside.

One of the guards nodded a wary greeting. They and their cats were always jumpiest at this time of day.

'Everything all right, officer?'

'Yeah. Call me crazy, but I think I just heard an elephant.'

When he and his puma were out of sight, I heaved the can of beans through Dr Grobe's lighted window.

'What the hell?' he shouted. I slipped back to my office, waited a few minutes, then went to see him.

A slender ray came through the broken window and struck the clock on the opposite wall. Grobe sat transfixed, staring at it with more surprise than ever. And no wonder, for the clock had become a parrot.

'Relax, Oddpork,' I said. 'It's only some funny kind of hologram in the clock face, worked by a laser from the lawn. You look like a comic villain, sitting there with that cigar stub in your face.'

The cigar stub moved. Looking closer, I saw it was made up of the packed tails of a few cockroaches, trying to force themselves between his closed lips. More ran up from his spotless collar and joined them, and others made for his nostrils. One approached the queue at the mouth, found another stuck there, and had a nibble at its kicking hind leg.

'Get away! Get away!' I gave Grobe a shake to dislodge them, and his mouth fell open. A brown flood of kicking bodies tumbled out and down, over his well-cut lapels.

I had stopped shuddering by the time I joined the others on the bluff. Pawlie and Blenheim were missing. Edna stopped scanning the horizon with her brass telescope long enough to introduce me to the pretty twins, Alice and Celia. They sat in the grass beside a tangled heap of revolvers, polishing their patent-leather tap shoes.

The ubiquitous Rastus was wiping off his burnt cork makeup. I asked him why.

'Don't need it anymore. Last night it was my camouflage. I was out in the woods, cutting a path through the electric fence. Quite a wide path, as you'll understand.'

He continued removing the black until I recognized the late George Hoad.

'George! But you cut your throat, remember? Mopping up blood—'

'Hank, that was your blood. It was you cut your throat in the Gents, After Pawlie vanished. Remember?'

'I did, giddily. 'What happened to you, then?'

'Your suicide attempt helped me make up my mind; I quit the Institute next day. You were still in the hospital.'

Still giddy, I turned to watch Joe Feeney operating the

curious laser I'd seen in the library. Making parrots out of clocks.

'I understand now,' I said. 'But what's the watermelon for?'

'Cheap cooling device.'

'And the "flag"?' I indicated the shawl-stick arrangement.

'To rally round. I stuck it in the melon because they were using the umbrella stand for—'

'Look!' Edna cried. 'The attack begins!' She handed me a second telescope.

All I saw below was the lone figure of Blenheim in his diving suit, shuffling slowly up from the river mist to face seven guards and two pumas. He seemed to be juggling croquet balls.

'Why don't we help him?' I shouted. 'Don't just sit there shining shoes and idling.'

The twins giggled. 'We've already helped some,' said Alice, nodding at the pile of weapons. 'We made friends with the guards.'

I got the point when those below pulled their guns on Blenheim. As each man drew, he looked at his gun and then threw it away.

'What a waste,' Celia sighed. 'Those guns are made from just about the best chocolate you can get.'

Blenheim played his parlour trick on the nearest guard: one juggled ball flew high, the guard looked up, and a second ball clipped him on the upturned chin.

Now the puma guards went into action.

'I can't look,' I said, my eye glued to the telescope. One of the animals stopped to sniff at a sticky revolver, but the other headed straight for his quarry. He leapt up, trying to fasten his claws into the stranger's big brass head.

Out of the river mist came a terrible cry, and then a terrible sight: a hobbling grey hulk that resolved into a charging elephant. Charging diagonally, so it looked even larger.

The pumas left the scene. One fled in our direction until Alice snatched up a pistol and fired it in the air. At that sound, the guards decided to look for jobs elsewhere. After all, as

Pawlie said later, you couldn't expect a man to face a juggling diver *and* a mad elephant with a wooden leg, with nothing but a chocolate .38, not on *those* wages.

Pawlie was riding on the neck of the elephant. When he came to a wobbling stop I saw that one of Jumbo's forelegs was a section of tree with the bark still on it. And in the bark, a heart with PS + HL, carved years before.

I felt the triumph was all over – especially since Pawlie kept nodding her head yes at me – until George said:

'Come on, gang. Let's set it up.'

Jumbo had been pulling a wooden sledge, bearing the Paris kiosk. Now he went off to break his fast on water and grass, while the rest of us set the thing upright. Even before we had fuelled it with whatever was in the fertilizer bags, I guessed that it was a rocket.

After some adjustments, the little door was let down, and a sweet, breakfast pancake odour came forth. Joe Feeney opened a flask of dark liquid and poured it in the entrance. The smell grew stronger.

'Maple sap,' he explained. 'From Jumbo's wooden leg. Mixed with honey. And there's oatmeal inside. A farewell breakfast.'

I looked in the little door and saw the inside of the ship was made like a metal honeycomb, plenty of climbing room for our masters.

Pawlie came from the building with a few cockroaches in a jar, and let them taste our wares. Then, all at once, it was a sale opening at any big department store. We all stood back and let the great brown wave surge forward and break over the little rocket. Some of them, nymphs especially, scurried all the way up to the nose cone and back down again in their excitement. It all looked so jolly that I tried not to think about their previous meals.

Edna glanced at her watch. 'Ten minutes more,' she said. 'Or they'll hit the sun.'

I objected that we'd never get all of them loaded in ten minutes.

'No,' said Pawlie, 'but we'll get the best and strongest. The shrews can keep the rest in control.'

Edna closed the door, and the twins did a vigorous tap-dance on the unfortunate stragglers. A few minutes later, a million members of the finest organization on earth were on their way to the stars.

'To join their little friends,' said Edna.

Pawlie and I touched hands, as Blenheim opened his face-plate.

'I've been making this study,' he said, 'of spontaneous combustion in giraffes . . .'

The Design

Andrews is to write a biography of Bruggs, the famous designer of bridges. Logically, the place to start would be with Oursler, a sociologist who was his best friend at school. But some quarrel in their youth made Oursler leave engineering, and estranged the two men for life. Andrews is reluctant to approach Oursler, and puts off interviewing him.

Instead he speaks to Bruggs' secretary, Priscilla, and to his aide, Chandler. Was the bachelor Bruggs intimate with his pretty secretary? No, he never made a pass, but he did act astonishingly jealous. Once, because she gave Chandler a small gift, Bruggs beat him and threw him down a flight of stairs.

The gift meant only that Priscilla felt sorry for poor Chandler, whose wife had cuckolded him with a middle-aged man named Rent. Doris Chandler flaunted her affair before her husband for over a year, then finally went to live with Rent in Switzerland. On a hunch, Andrews goes to see them, hoping they can clear up the rumored connection of Bruggs with a gambling czar named Gordon.

Rent is an old, withered person whose only living heir is his stepson, Reverend Queen. Queen finds it scandalous that his stepfather should be suspected, as he is, of murdering the Zurich banker, Straud.

Doris now works for a Swiss lawyer named Enderby, who is also a suspect in the Straud case. Enderby is the mentor and kindly advisor of still a third suspect, the youthful and homosexual Trell. The lawyer visits him daily.

Interviewing Trell, Andrews learns that Enderby has been using his visits to the young man to see Trell's sister Fran. It is evident that Enderby loves her, yet, perhaps because he is her brother's legal guardian, he does not declare it.

Andrews learns more of Fran from her close friend and confidant, the mannish actress, Victoria Staton. While admitting she had once a lesbian flirtation with Fran's sister Ursula, 'Victorio', as she calls herself, protests she has only platonic regard for Fran herself.

Fran is now deep in debt to Gordon, head of the gambling syndicate. Victoria has already made one unsuccessful attempt to assassinate him. Now he is in Paris, trying to persuade one Irma Hathaway to become his mistress. Andrews finds him.

Gordon says little of the others, but denies he wants Irma Hathaway for a mistress. He wants only to find out more about her; is she, like Victoria, a British spy? Assisting him is the woman he loves, Hera, who is spying on Irma, posing as a maid.

Back in Switzerland, Andrews learns that Irma is indeed an agent, but she is working for the American, Johnson. He phones Johnson, who invites him over for the weekend.

Ursula is present, and Johnson informs everyone that he is her real father. Now he feigns homosexuality, flirting with the young Russian Ursula loves, Yoniski. Yoniski has brought along his sister Kathia, and when he fails with the brother, Johnson pretends passion for this armless girl. No one is fooled by Johnson, and finally he tells the truth – that he is married to Victoria Staton, and loves her.

Kathia and her brother have come to Switzerland with their father, the well-known physicist Xerov, who believes he has cancer. He wishes to consult the popular specialist, Linder.

Unannounced, Dr Linder appears, full of good humor and anecdotes. Some days past, he says, he was approached by a man named Menkov, a secret police agent who had trailed Xerov from Moscow and lost him at the airport in Berne. He suspected Linder knew Xerov's whereabouts, and offered a considerable bribe for the information. Ironically, Xerov is quite well physically, though 'neutrotic squared', says Dr Linder. 'Neurotic cubed.' But it is Menkov who has the cancer. Linder persuaded him to try surgery, and now Menkov is in the local hospital, only three rooms (though he doesn't know it) from the malingering Xerov.

To Andrews, Menkov confesses he has become the protector of a young girl named Wendy, an orphan who has also become a suspect in the Straud murder. He brought up the child under great difficulty, being utterly ignored by his wealthy cousin in London, Nora Chamberlin. Nora detests children and animals, but likes machines. Her only friend, as far as Menkov knows, is Priscilla, Bruggs' secretary.

In London, Andrews meets Nora, a great red-faced angry woman who once had a barroom brawl with Rent's heir, young Reverend Queen. Nora is now engaged in suing Priscilla for 'alienation of Bruggs' affections', though she has never commanded them. She refuses to talk any more to Andrews, or to anyone but her friend, Oursler.

Andrews realizes he must rely on the sociologist's information. He telephones Priscilla and asks if she would like to go with him to see Oursler, but she wants no contact with any enemy of Bruggs. Finally Andrews calls Oursler, who promises to come to see him the same evening.

The evening newspaper contains another turn of the screw: Xerov, against the protests of his son, invites little Wendy to visit him in the hospital. He locks his son in a closet and tries to rape the orphan, but Wendy is saved by Reverend Queen. Now Xerov and Yoniski have been added to the list of the suspected murderers of Straud.

Who killed Straud? There are no clues to the stabbing, and each of the six suspects (Enderby, Rent, Wendy, Xerov, Yoniski and Trell) has plenty of motive and opportunity.

In trying to puzzle it out on a piece of paper, Andrews comes up with an interesting diagram of the relationships of the people he has met. It looks like a bridge, with missing braces.

DS seems to indicate that Doris is yet another suspect for Straud's death, so Andrews adds that brace.

Oursler comes into the room, notices the paper on the desk, and laughs. 'It was not a good design,' he says, 'but it was mine.

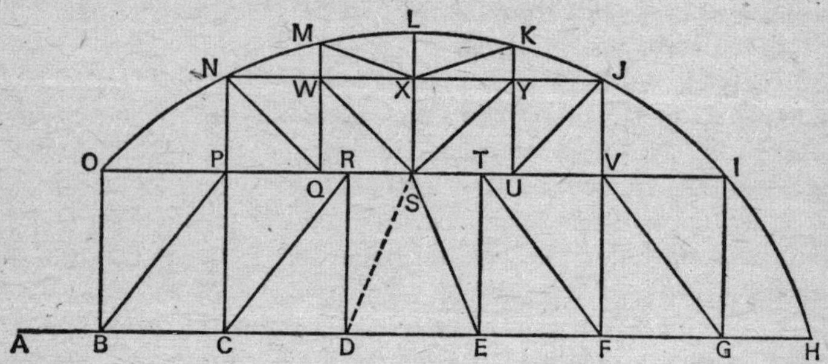

Bruggs stole it from me, back in engineering school, fifty years ago. Now I have it back.'

He takes a gun from his pocket, hesitates, then shoots Andrews. Andrews tries to speak the name of his ex-wife, Hera, but no sound comes. He dies. Oursler draws OA.

The Face

God hath given you one face, and you make yourselves another

I must try to tell this impartially, with a scientific concern for truth. It is not my story, after all. I played only a small part at the end.

Yet the end, in a way, returns to the beginning. This story is a snake swallowing its own tail.

Is the tape recording? My name is James P. Anderson, and I am – was a lab technician working for the special project. My work was trivial, for I have very little formal scientific training.

Not that I'm ignorant. You pick up things, here and there. I've been reading about the lives of great scientists. I know, for one thing, how Auguste Kekulé discovered the chemical structure of benzene. Not too many chemists know that. He found it in a dream.

I keep dreaming that someone is trying to tear off my face. The doctor says that's just the healing and tightening of new tissue, nothing to worry about.

Kekulé dreamed of snakes, circling and biting their own tails. That's how he discovered the benzene ring. Snakes . . .

The three boys who found the object in Hill Park were, they say, hunting for garter snakes. The Barnes boy said that at first they all thought the object was a rubber mask lying in the grass. But his friends said they knew at once that it was 'something weird'. What is the truth here?

They experimented, trying to turn it over with sticks. They bruised it, and scratched the cheek, which bled. Barnes and Schmidt later claimed it was the third boy, Dalston, who committed 'most' of these injuries. By way of appeasement, they brought the object offerings of fresh flowers. Finally Barnes told his parents. Barnes senior, a water inspector, visited the site and immediately called the police.

The police report speaks of the object as 'face of a partly-buried Caucasian, sex unknown'. According to the medical examiner, the person was unconscious: 'Respiration shallow, estimated temperature subnormal, pulse slow. Pupils dilated. The mouth could not be opened.'

The discovery was unusual enough for the evening papers, who headlined it as *Live Burial Mystery.* A few reporters hung around the site, waiting for the police to uncover the rest of the supposed person.

A few minutes after the digging started, it stopped. The police held a whispered conference and then cleared the reporters from the area. That night they put up steel barriers and canvas screens.

Newsmen could only guess at what was happening by the comings and goings of important men: city officials, army officers and medical specialists. The morning papers guessed wildly that the buried person was a spy, a 'living bomb', a plague victim. In the evening editions, the story was killed.

It was killed in this case by unofficial pressure – friendly phone calls from certain government offices to city editors. For this reason, reporters felt free to continue chasing down leads.

One man (Cobb of the *Sentinel*) made two discoveries that led in the right direction. He talked to a homicide detective who admitted being puzzled by the undisturbed grass around the face. In his opinion, no one had been digging there for months.

Secondly, a park gardener said he was surprised to hear of a burial in that spot, high on the side of the hill.

'The soil's thin there,' he said. 'Bedrock's only three or four inches down.'

Cobb continued digging. He asked the boys if they'd noticed anything unusual, when they'd found the face. Two hadn't, and the Schmidt boy (obviously enjoying his sudden fame) now recalled noticing all too much: The face had a third eye, it gave off an eerie blue glow, there was human blood on the lips, etc., etc.

Finally, Cobb talked to one of the rescue workers who'd been digging for the body.

'Everywhere we went down, we struck rock. I didn't know it was rock right away, I thought maybe the guy was wearing a suit of armor or something, see? Anyway, I went down around the head, and more rock. I says, Hell, where is the rest of this guy?

'So then I got down with a trowel, cleared the soil around the head, and got my hand under it, see, to lift it up. So I'm like this, see, with my right hand under the head, and my left on the face. I can feel the guy's breath on the back of my hand. I start to lift, and then I look.

'I couldn't believe it. I can feel the guy's breath. I'm lifting, and I'm looking right where the guy's brain ought to be. And I'm seeing a handful of roots and dirt, with slugs and things crawling around in it. *There's no back to his head.* Just a face!'

Slugs and things. Any chance of heading off public hysteria was now gone. Wire services repeated Cobb's story, heating it up. Within hours, police and army spokesmen had denied it, confirmed it and refused to comment. The medical examiner cleared his throat and admitted to sixty million viewers that, well, yes, he would have to say the face was alive, in a way. Medically speaking. Well, yes, it was breathing. And no, he had no explanation at the moment. But the experts were no doubt looking into it . . .

The *experts*? How many experts could there be on bodiless, living faces? Within days, however, there were dozens of expert opinions in the air. A botanist said the thing was no human face at all, but a peculiar species of mushroom. (He hadn't actually seen it when he said this.) A famous plastic surgeon spoke of little-known advances in transplants. A zoologist spoke of protective camouflage. A religious leader mentioned the imprint of Christ's face on the veil of Veronica. Everyone spoke of the veil of secrecy that was keeping back the truth from the public.

In time, the government allowed a few photos to be published. The face was variously identified as Lincoln, Gandhi, Martin Bormann, Amelia Earhart . . .

By now citizens in every part of the nation were spotting faces in their back yards, especially in the shadows of foliage. Others scanned the sky and found faces in the clouds, which they connected with the imminent flying-saucer invasion. Unscrupulous or uncaring magazines dug up the fantasies of the Schmidt boy. By the end of the month, even the newsmen were getting tired of calls from spirit media ('I have contacted the Face by ouija. It is Christian and vegetarian . . .'), from pranksters ('Listen, I got this nose growing in my window box . . .') and from prophets of doom. One day the *Sentinel* editor threw out letters from three people claiming the face as their own, one man from Mars, and one man who explained that the face was controlling his thoughts by means of a 'death dream laser'. The editor then wrote an open letter asking for a special Presidential Commission to investigate:

> We've had enough of official silence and scientific double-talk. The public is concerned and alarmed. The only way to put a stop to these crank letters and Halloween-mask hoaxes, is to answer these questions: What is the Face? Where did it come from? How did it get planted in the park? Is it human and conscious? Can it speak? Can it think?

Actually a special project was already set up to investigate the object. Not appointed by the President or Congress (who were probably afraid of looking foolish), but by the Office of Naval Research jointly with University Hospital. As a lab technician from the hospital, I played a humble part in the project. My duties were washing glassware and reading dials. Dull work, yes, but necessary. A vital part of the search for truth.

I arrived in town the day of the open letter. I cut it out of the *Sentinel* and pinned it on my wall at 'home'. I intended to check off the editor's questions one by one, as we found the answers.

'Home' for now was a disused Army barracks on the edge of

the city, where most of the staff were quartered. I pinned up the letter and took a bus straight to Hill Park, hoping to glimpse the object itself. I didn't even stop to unpack, which is why I forgot to bring my pass.

It was a warm June day, 27°C. Most of the people on my bus seemed to be headed for the beach. As I later learned, most of them had no jobs to go to. I stepped off the bus and stood shading my eyes to look up at the hill in Hill Park. Near the top they were setting up the metal walls of our laboratory. The park gates were closed, and guarded by two Marines. Too late, I remembered the pass in my suitcase.

As I stood there, a man wearing a white armband with crude lettering on it handed me a leaflet.

'I haven't got any change,' I said.

'It's free,' he said. 'Read it, mister. Find out what the Face really means. Come to our rally tonight and hear the truth.'

'The truth?'

'The *real* truth. Not what these government bastards want us to believe. The truth they're afraid of.'

I didn't tell him I was working for the government bastards; it would only have provoked him. He stared at me until I smiled and put the leaflet in my pocket. I forgot all about it for the time being.

From the window of the bus back to the barracks, I saw several wall graffiti I didn't understand. But they all seemed to refer to the object. One was a face divided by a bolt of lightning. One was a face surrounded by sun rays. I remember these two only because I've seen them so often since, but there were many others. The object in the park had already become the focus of several movements, both political and mystical. Most of them, like the Society of the Peaceful Face, the American Vigilante Volunteers and the Space Brotherhood, either disbanded or merged, but anyhow dropped out of sight. Only two evolved and lived on.

The Guardians of the Mask emphasized the fact that the object was a *white* face. They believed it to be only part of the body to come. Any day now, the hands would turn up in, say, Britain, and the feet in Scandinavia, and the rest in other Caucasian countries. (Medical students often played cruel tricks with these pathetic hopes.) Finally the complete Messiah–Fuhrer would assemble himself and lead them into the final, racial Armageddon, in which all but the white race would certainly die.

The New Universologists on the other hand believed the object to be an oracle. They reckoned it had now been sleeping for nearly a thousand years. Soon it would awaken, to tell them what to do next, to achieve a world of lasting peace and brotherhood.

Normally both movements might have appealed only to a fringe of unhappy people, but these were far from normal times. The nation was undergoing great economic and political upheavals, and the government almost daily proved itself unequal to the problems of unemployment and unrest. Both movements attracted thousands in this city alone, and perhaps hundreds of thousands more were sympathetic to their causes. Other cities were close behind.

The Communist Party saw which way the wind blew, and lent some support to the New Universologists (NU), to help them organize. In return, over the next few months, the NU began to lay more stress on workers' control of industry, and less on miracles. Reacting, ultra-conservative groups threw in their lot – and their considerable money – with the Guardians of the Mask (GM). Up and down the country there were demonstrations and counter-demonstrations, rallies and rally-smashers, protest marches and torchlight processions. And a sense of urgency. A sense that power was now within reach of those who most needed it. Power was just inside the gates of Hill Park.

Or so they must have thought. At different times, both groups tried storming the park to rescue their idol. The police, even with state police reinforcements, were almost overwhelmed by the second attack. Next day the edge of the park was barricaded with sandbags, and several hundred Marines were billeted inside. From now on until the end of our project, no one could ever be allowed to come into the park.

The end of our project? It dragged its long, slow, serpent's body through the summer, with no end in sight. One day in October I looked up at the news clipping on my wall. Not a single vital question had been answered. We knew nothing important, and it looked as though we never would. Our work had disintegrated into endless proofs and disproofs of secondary theories. The serpent had no end, it had swallowed it, and now chewed on itself . . .

Who am I, a lab technician, to make this judgement? I speak, not of the scientific facts, but of the human differences within the project. I wasn't just washing glassware and reading dials, not all the time. I kept my eyes open.

There was a fundamental split from the very beginning, between Dr Lowell, our project director, and Dr Grauber, head of the medical section. The medical people wanted to move the object to University Hospital and place it under intensive care. Dr Lowell supported the biologists who argued against this, saying that it might be dangerous to uproot it from its present environment. Dr Grauber replied that this was entirely a medical decision, hence his to make. Dr Lowell said that depended entirely on whether or not the object was truly human.

'How on earth can we find out what it is unless we get it into a proper laboratory? Do you expect my men to do biopsies out *here*?' Grauber had to stand on tiptoe to shout this into Lowell's face. The director was a head taller than Grauber, and, like many big men, bland and almost friendly in an argument. He liked to pose as a big, jolly, absent-minded professor, slow of speech and always fishing for his pipe in one pocket of his baggy tweed jacket. In reality he was a ruthless executive. Whatever he knew or didn't know about science, he knew how to command. Most of us came to respect him, even like him.

Grauber was generally unliked. I knew him from the hospital, where they called him Napoleon. A cold, logical little man, a brilliant scientist, but he threw tantrums when he didn't get his way.

He tore off his pince-nez and shook them under Lowell's nose – as though he wanted to shake a fist at him. 'Is that what you expect? Is it? Is it?'

Lowell sighed. 'Dr Grauber, I expect you to follow my direction. We'll get along better if you do, okay?'

It was not okay. The arguments grew worse as the project dragged on through the summer. The staff were all upset; we all found ourselves taking sides. I would hear:

'Grauber just wants to get control of the project himself. So he wants to drag the thing off to his own lab, and then gradually ease Lowell out of the driver's seat. I've seen his kind before.'

'Are you crazy? Grauber's ten times the scientist Lowell ever will be. And I'll tell you something else. He really cares about that "thing" out there. It's no "thing" to him, it's a human being in need of medical treatment.'

There was something in both sides; I didn't know what to believe. After one shattering evening of this, I quit work early. I had to drag myself on the bus, and then I sat with closed eyes, wishing away my throbbing headache. The engine vibration and bright lights were still getting through to me, so finally I got out and walked.

It was quiet and dark. Just my footsteps and the occasional streetlight. I noticed my headache going.

Then I turned a corner and found myself at a rally of the New Universologists. There were maybe fifty people listening, and one white-haired man speaking from the back of a pickup truck. The banner behind him said THE FACE OF PEACE, and showed the sun-ray symbol. Most of the people looked poor, but more or less respectable. One exception was the dirty, unshaven man who was taking pictures.

'. . . a face of peace,' said the speaker. 'Brothers, do you know what peace means? Do any of us know? Have they ever let us find out? Not a chance.

'Of course peace will be hard on some people. Think of all those rich arms manufacturers that'll have to go out and get an honest job! Think of all the generals who might have to work for a living! Think of the paid-off politicians who get a piece of every big arms contract – on relief! We all know who's against peace, don't we? *And they've got a steel ring around Hill Park right now!*

'What are they so afraid of, brothers? I'll tell you . . .'

But he never did tell us, for just then a man in a Halloween mask jumped up and pulled him down off the truck. There were more men in masks with baseball bats, hitting people in the front of the crowd.

Someone screamed, 'The GMs!'

We ran. I looked back from a safe distance. Two of the invaders were kicking the white-haired man as he lay in the street. Others were trying to turn over the truck. My headache was back, and now I felt sick to my stomach besides.

At work the Grauber–Lowell arguments went on. Medical staff monitored the object's temperature, pulse and respiration (dials for me to read), all below normal. They took tissue samples (a biopsy) and found it had human flesh. Radiologists found that the face contained normal human face bones and teeth. The jaw was fused, unworkable. Three of the teeth had metal fillings. All this enabled Grauber to say:

'It's human, for God's sake! It's in a coma. Probably dying!'

'*Part*-human,' Lowell replied, lighting his pipe. 'A symbiosis, I think. And we're in a unique position to study it in its natural environment. Let's not plop it in a hospital bed just yet, shall we?'

And there was evidence for his side, too. The back of the object was connected to the soil through masses of tiny thread-like roots. Vegetation seemingly living in symbiosis with a human face. Just how the two worked together was unclear. An ultrasonic probe showed clusters of tiny sacs attached to some of these roots. The sacs pulsated together, providing the object's pseudo-breathing.

Everyone took sides but me. I tried hard to stay impartial, to wait for the final blaze of truth. At home I tried not to notice the yellowed clipping on the wall. None of the questions were checked off. We knew nothing.

The last week of October was the worst. Dr Grauber said

that the first frost might kill the object, whether or not it was human. Dr Lowell agreed, but argued for moving it to a greenhouse, not a hospital. All over town there were cryptic notices of a massive GM procession, on Halloween, 'Night of the Mask'. Police leave was cancelled for that night, and still more Marines were brought in. When I arrived for work at dusk, I saw them setting up machine guns on the barricades. *Ring of steel*, I thought. *And for what?*

Someone said Dr Grauber wanted to see me. While I waited outside his office I could hear him and Lowell arguing.

'You admit you know nothing of medicine, Dr Lowell. You're a biologist. A marine biologist at that. You know about as much about medicine as I know about – pogonophorae.'

'Certainly. But I don't see—'

'Then I'll spell it out for you. The face is human, or part-human. If he dies, because you've disregarded medical advice – good advice – that's murder.'

'Oh, come now. You can't—'

'I can. I'll have you arrested, Dr Lowell. And brought to trial.'

'You'll never prove it's human.'

'No, you'll probably get off. But think of the headlines. Think of what the publicity will mean to your precious career.'

'God damn you,' said Lowell pleasantly. 'I almost think you would, too. Still, I can always fire you.'

There was a loud click. When Lowell came out, he was putting the broken pieces of his pipe in his pocket. He looked worried, but when he saw me, he smiled.

'Next patient,' he said.

Grauber looked sick. He was polishing his pince-nez furiously, perhaps to disguise the trembling of his hands.

'Ah, Anderson is it?' He never remembered the names or faces of his staff. 'Sit down, Anderson. I have some rather bad news for you.'

I sat down. 'What is it, Doctor?'

'The FBI came to see me earlier, to tell me you're a security risk.'

'What? Me?'

'They showed me a photograph of you at some rally. One of these odd-ball groups that keeps trying to smash their way into the park. And they searched your room at the barracks and found a certain leaflet.'

'But I can explain—'

He held up a hand. 'I'm sure you can. I'm sure you can. But not to me. I don't understand these new political things. *They* say you must go, so go you must. I am sorry. Of course we'll try to keep you on at the hospital, if we can. I'm sure you mean us no harm.'

'No harm? No *harm*?' When I got outside, I had to laugh. It's said Auguste Kekulé laughed when he awoke from his dream to understand the benzene ring. In the words of the song:

Then I awoke
Was this some kind of joke?

It was, and the joke was on me. I had worked four months for the project, washing glassware, reading dials. Keeping an open mind, not taking sides. Waiting for the blaze of truth. And the truth was *I had never laid eyes on the Face itself*.

Well, now was the time. Coming up the hill to the park I could see the great GM procession, thousands on thousands of tiny lights like the glittering scales of one huge snake. Pointing to the truth in the park. Over there, in that little tent. What would they do, if they broke in? Carry it away? Fall down and worship, pressing their hideous masks to the ground? Too many questions (Can it speak? Can it think?), and no answers.

I thought of Kekulé's dream again. Was there another meaning? The snake devours its tail: All things must turn back to their origins. The circle is zero. Ashes to ashes . . .

I took a 500 ml bottle of benzene from the lab, where I had used it to clean the glassware. Kekulé's benzene, the big zero. When I tore open the flaps of the little tent I could hardly make out the Face. Just a lighter oval in the darkness. I poured the bottle of benzene on it and ignited it. They tell me there was an explosion. My face was burned, and I have lost my sight.

But I have seen enough.

The Master Plan

SH (Yes, that was a kind of command: QUIET–HOSPITAL ZONE. The General's dry eyes flicker, and he lets them close against the fluorescent whiteness.

He stands naked in the corridor, swaying slightly. When he opens his eyes he sees that the light has robbed him of his shadow. A little more gloom, he complains reasonably. And some eerie Muzak, please. (*Miss R. B. Glaski and Miss T. N. Nye were his two-day nurses. The punning part of his backbrain relabelled them Miss Glass and Miss Nylon, and then went on to further barbarisms: Intern Al Hemorrhage, etc. Only the surgeon, Dr Godden, seemed to escape.*

One night the General awoke with a high fever **(The subject was born in Avalon, Iowa, in 1925, and there lived with both parents (and an older sister) until 1944, when drafted into the Army Air Force. The subject married Miss Ruth Matthias in 1946. Their only child, a boy, died at birth two years later.**

Attended the following schools: University of Minnesota (USAFROTC), 1946–50: B.S. (Math.) Fort Buechner Flight School, Amis, Texas, 1951–2. The War College Annexe, Port Smith, Virginia: M.S., Ph.D. The Air Defense Academy, Casper, Wyoming, 1958–9. L'Ecole Supérieure de la Science Militaire, Antwerp, 1966.

The subject is an Associate Fellow of the Potomac Institute for Advanced Studies, Washington, D.C. (*It may seem presumptuous to call the Master Plan both beautifully simple and elegant, but such is done in the certain* *knowledge that it is the only means of carrying on wars of any kind whatever; that it will supersede everything from the meanest counterinsurgency campaign to the most ambitious and brilliant global showdown. The Plan is a complete, self-contained system of programming which does not admit of lesser plans. Strategy and tactics are drawn into its circle of radiance and there transmuted.* *(In his room with the door shut, and The Lone Ranger turned up loud. Even then, he could hear Dad shouting at her. She'd be better off dead than coming to him like this. He'd rather kill any daughter of his who came home in trouble. The razor blade slipped through the sheet of balsa and into his finger and right out again. (ITEM* **DESCRIPTION :** (He was late to work at the hybrid seed corn plant, so now he had to drive through the late-maze that must be insoluble. 'They're making a movie of my life,' he explained to the doctor. 'It must be in the next room, but I think it's too late to see it.' 'On TV,' the doctor said, motioning him to the second butcher's block. On the first lay an oddly familiar figure, split open. It lay face down, like someone making love. The cleaver) *Blood the color of dirty brick fell to the razor-nicked edge of the table. 'Hi-yo, Silver!')* **The subject was a jet ace twice in Korea, and was awarded the DFC in 1953. Later that year, the subject suffered a nervous collapse, and was retired from flight duty.)** *conscious of a presence by the bed. Ruth? Out of the question – the night nurse, maybe. He did not roll over to look, but held himself rigid. After awhile, he slept again. Dreamlessly.*

The next morning Captain Savage made the first of his many little visits. He was not only attached to the General's staff, he was for the moment the entire staff, his only link with the Pentagon. The two set about preparing the General's monograph on the Master Plan.

Captain Savage was a fussy, pedantic little clerk, complete to the pair of silver-rimmed glasses gripping his nose like calipers. His sharp face grew animated when he was talking of numbers, and his hands – when they were not making a priestly gesture, fingertips together – were forever busy counting and naming things.

His briefcase contained only a silver writing instrument, a blank note pad, and the scrambler tape recorder.

(In October, 1960, Ruth née Matthias filed for divorce from her husband on the grounds of mental cruelty. A month later, she dropped this suit. In December, 1960, she committed suicide by barbiturates. Her note is reproduced in full:

> **This is it, big ace. Cram your Air Force. I've had it. I know you'll be happy to be rid of me, so you can marry Helen. At least this is one way I'll get away from the Air Force, Kiss me goodbye, dear. Be good. You've never loved me for a minute, or anything else but your magic squares or whatever they are. I want you to enjoy yourself, your few last years, with Helen. By the way ace, the doctor phoned. He says he thinks you've got cancer.**

The note was pronounced genuine, after computer analysis by the Schneidman system, having the following characteristics:

1. **Specific information.**
2. **Names of people, places, concrete things.***
3. **Frequent mention of a man.**
4. **Gave instructions to others that were concrete enough to be carried out.**
5. **Fewer percentage of THINK words.**
6. **Greater percentage of actions by a man upon the writer.**
7. **Mention of the word 'love'.**

***Although the name 'Helen' does not seem to refer to a real person.**

The following year, the subject underwent successful surgery for removal of a benign brain

tumor. In 1966, a second tumor was removed from the colon. Within a few months, a malignancy was discovered in the region of the thyroid gland. The presence of a second growth in the brain was suspected, and in 1968 the subject entered Atwater Clinic for observation.

(THE BURAC 8800 SERIES COMPUTERS. This series, having been found useful for previous contingency theory operations, was selected for the Master Plan. Special, more highly flexible programming procedures were devised. To illustrate:

THE CHASE. Define a classic chase or hunt situation in which hunter A moves across the streets of a city in a car. He may make only right-angle turns, only at proper corners, and moves n blocks per second. The hunted, B, may move in any direction, not only keeping to the streets, but at a slower rate n—m blocks per second. At time t=O, B makes his presence known to A at some point (x_{OB}, y_{OB})*, while A is at some other point* (x_{OA}, y_{OA})*. A is blind to B's movements, if any, after this time. The classic problem is to catch B in the shortest possible time. Assuming B's path to be completely random, this is a simple time series problem, and a solution is possible.*

But suppose B able to transport himself instantaneously from any point to any other. Suppose he is able to disappear entirely for any finite duration. Suppose that he is able to move in three dimensions, or some higher number. Classical anaylsis is unable to deal with these processes. But the Master Plan may deal with these and many other contingencies, including the unlikely possibility that B becomes A himself (hiding by identity)!

(He kept a diary, marking certain days with asterisks. In the summer he went detasseling, and the slippery sex organs of the male hybrid seed corn cut into his hands. The older boys smoked corn silk rolled up in newspaper. They asked him if he knew what a blanket party without a blanket was called. Peace on earth was the answer, and when he failed to laugh, they turned away, disgusted by his ignorance.

(ITEM DESCRIPTION:

1. WOMAN, Human, self-propelled, four-limbed, objective, interesting, sexually
2. not applicable
3. n/a.

(movie, in some other language, showed the three-year-old General tossing a stick into Fox Lake for Blackie to retrieve. The General wore his striped coveralls with the red rubber buttons he dared not touch. Blackie swam out and never came back.

'Something,' something said, 'has been let out of the cataloged ode ran:' and showed him the neat ranks of code letters.

AA=T	BA=M	CA=W	DA=P
AB=H	BB=Y	CB=O	DB=D
AC=I	BC=E	CC=A	DC=.
AD=S	BD=N	CD=L	DD=/

AAABACADDDACADDDBABBDDBCBDBCBA
BBDDACBDDDCAABCBBADDACDDCCBADD
CABCCDCDDDDACDBCCCADBCDBDDDC

He solved it without the key, but it was late, for work. The sound of the grindstone sharpening the cleaver, became the drone of medium bombers coming in over the lake.)

The last day of detasseling season he fought one of the biggest boys and won, although his cut lip developed a lump that lasted far into the winter – long after his blue jeans stopped smelling of sweat and pollen.

When the war began, the town put up a Roll of Honor on Courthouse Square. For a time, the sign painter had to come every day, ruling it with his blue chalk line and sketching in the names of the dead.)

The contingencies involved in a single battle plan are of course staggering. If each of two opposing generals has merely fifteen decisions to make, each decision comprising two choices, the number of possible battles is over a billion. To investigate all of them would take some time. And even the simplest bush action requires hundreds of quick decisions, inter-related in obscure ways, and multivalent.)

The third week, he asked Savage how the scrambler tape recorder worked.

'It's sealed, you see.' The captain named one finger. 'Any attempt to open it will set off a charge which vaporizes its thin-film components.' He moved to the second finger.

'Part of it generates a signal of unknown shape which is mixed with your speech and the resultant signal recorded.'

On the Masonic signet finger, he said, 'The REWIND button operates a destruct mechanism. There can be no rewinding or erasing.'

Pinky. 'To prevent the accumulation of a large amount of material and solution of the signal, the signal shape is changed with each new tape cartridge. This button does it.'

'How's your sex life?'

'Sir?'

'Let's get on with it.' The machine went on. 'To begin with, let me repeat what I said at the start: It is not enough *for a plan to cover all contingencies. It must* also *be the simplest possible solution, and it must be beautiful – elegant, if you like. It must have the beauty of a dream: utterly strange, but* THE RIGHT PLACE. *When I see a good plan, something tells me* I'VE BEEN HERE BEFORE.'

Beaming Dr Godden came in to draw some more blood. He sat on the edge of the bed, smoothing the skirts of his white coat. Flashing a penlight in the General's eyes, he asked him how we were feeling this morning. The General did not reply.

Abruptly the doctor put away the toy and forced his face from its molded smile for a moment. 'We have the biopsy report on you, General, I'm afraid it's positively malignant. We'd like to try a little exploratory surgery, but of course I'm afraid there's nothing – in cases like these, one can't hold out too much—'

'Don't get so broken up about it, Doctor. You must handle a dozen or so terminal cancer patients a year, yeah? So let's not

piss our britches over one more or less.' The General showed his teeth.

'I'm glad you're resigned. However—'

'I'm far from resigned. I'm scared to hell, but there isn't anything I can do now but die. Except for my work.'

'Your work?'

'I want to have enough time to finish this monograph. As long as I'm sane enough, logical enough, I want to go on with it. So no pain-killers. I don't want anything dulling my brain or shortening my life by a single minute, hear?'

The doctor rose, smiling assent, but behind that smile was another, which said: 'You poor son of a bitch, you think you can get along without it, do you? A week or two from now, you're going to be begging for the needle, just like everyone else. And I, healer, physician, Christlike friend, will of course hear your plea, I may even "help you across", if you ask me nice . . . we often get such requests . . .'

'Where was I?' he asked Savage.

'. . . the beauty of a dream, General.'

(hoped the faceless code-clerk would not turn around. His androgynous father/mother helped him into the rear of the plane, where pretty Miss Glass was already treating the burned child. The medics joking and loitering around the door were drunk. 'Peace on earth, get it? Don't you get it?' Miss Glass began peeling away the bandage roughly. The child screamed. The men began singing 'When the Khe San Goes Rolling Along', then 'Unter-der-Lyndon'. He could see pieces of the burned flesh coming away in the bandage. The singing drowned the screams. One of the medics staggered over and offered the molten face a Hershey bar.)

'Gentlemen, before we get into the work, I'm reminded of a story – a geographic story, naturally.' The class had permission to laugh with the colonel. 'They say a woman at different ages is like the seven continents' – he thought of Miranda the changeable, kissing him goodbye at the train. He'd wondered how they looked to others, and peered

around, but no one was watching them. Off We Go, Into The Wild Blue Yonder, the band played. A frantic, drunken soldier lurched to the train window and vomited into the bell of the tuba. Miranda promised to write, but never did – 'then she is like North America: fully explored and free with her resources.') *Plan must do exactly what a good general himself does:*

1. *Collect intelligence.*
2. *Outline a tentative plan of action, with reasonably accessible alternatives.*
3. *Feed in data from past personal and historical experiences.*
4. *Compute probable success of each operation.*
5. *Re-cast the original plan in terms of maximizing success.*
6. *Feed in newer intelligence, and reassess.*
7. *Repeat steps 4 through 6 as often as needed.*

To do all this, it has been necessary to equip the computer with immense amounts of historical and personal 'experience'. It is particularly important to clarify the vague notions of historians, and to break down the 'hunches' of line officers into analytical operations.

But there remained a further step: developing the scope and predictive ability of the Master Plan, by postulating novel situations and strategies to meet them.)

Psychologically, the subject seems relatively stable and integrated. The TAT shows a high ratio of paranoid fears and compulsive-obsessive enumeration to other characteristics. The MMPI profile showed paranoia more than two standard deviations above the norm, but the lie scale was too excessive to permit significant results. The subject has an I.Q. within the 170–200 range, with 70% certainty.)

'My own life is in a way an example of failure to consider contingencies,' he said. Savage leaned forward, ferret-eager. 'I begin to have bloody thoughts. My marriage has failed, and now my health. It would be pleasant, very pleasant, to blame all

this on The Enemy. But ultimately, the responsibility is mine. *If I could not avert these catastrophes, I could at least have prepared for them.'*

'You have an encyclopedic mind, General.'

'It isn't enough to be encyclopedic.' He breathed hard from pain. 'An encyclopedia is a miz-maze – I mean a mish-mash – of loose facts and opinions. A man must order his world completely. That's what life's all about.'

Life *was a magazine Miss Nylon read, or pretended to* read, *near the window on rainy days. She was just out of nursing school, and obviously getting over an unhappy affair. Who else could sigh over* Life's *pretty pages?*

Watching her tight little ass, the General considered offering her what he would call depth therapy. He decided against it for two reasons: (a) it would upset her small, unstable ethical system to board this sinking hulk; she would feel guilty when he was gone. (b) anything that could shorten his pain-shot life by even a second was foolish now, with the end of his work in sight.

He contented himself with the kind of Hollywood-battle-wound-ward flirtation he knew Miss N. could accommodate:
HE: (pinches her buttock)
SHE: (slaps his hand) You old goat, you!
HE: (touches her leg at hemline)
SHE: (slaps his hand) Naughty little boy!
HE: But you're so sexy!
SHE: And you *are just plain oversexed!*
HE: If I were thirty years younger, etc. etc.

The pain dreams intruded often now (His opposite number was General X, a fat Chinese sitting incredibly heavily on his chest. 'They are showing a chest x-ray of you in the other room,' he said. From under the tightly-closed door to the other room came a sudden gush of dark blood. 'My eyes!'))))) *and the occasional dullness of his mind was additional pain.)*

The two frightened nurses face him, uncertain whether or not to block his path. The boyish intern crouches near them in a fighter's stance. The figure on the floor is Dr Godden. The instrument in the naked General's hand is a surgical knife.

'This is my body,' he wants to gargle at them. 'I know none of you *believes* in the body. And how could you, hacking away at it day after bloody day?

'I say to you, I am your Frankenstein. You put me together in England, and on the surface the parts matched perfectly. But inside there was an ugly twist, an interface of artist's hand and murderer's wrist. Do you appreciate that these medical experiments cannot go on any longer? These Jewish women, kashered by the tens of thousands on your hospitassembly lines – *verstehen Sie? (The headaches and backaches were horribly constant. He became suddenly jaundiced and went on baby foods* *('Between forty and fifty, she is like Asia: Worn out but exotic. And finally, after fifty, she is like Australia: Everybody knows it's down there, but nobody gives a damn.').*

Interviewed, the subject demonstrated lack of affect regarding the death of Ruth ('She got what she wanted, I guess.' 'The marriage was a mistake. I'm sorry I made it, as I always am when I figure things out badly.') Was reticent about father ('anal-sadistic, I guess you'd jargon him. I'll say no more.') and mother ('a non-entity. I'm interested in entities.'), and under the strong delusion that a great discovery of some sort was imminent.)

If the following example appears vaguely worded and incomprehensible, it is merely to demonstrate the kind of problem the Master Plan is now learning to deal with. The author of this monograph apologizes, but prefers to skip over less interesting examples and come to grips with an essential one: The nature of The Enemy.

The Enemy is no one; is someone; is everyone. The Enemy is nowhere; somewhere; everywhere. He is without: within. The Enemy is myself.

These comprise a working vocabulary of statements the truth of which can be tested against various hypotheses. One may construct a hypothetical story, such as the following:

'I, Brig. Gen. Bernard Parks, USAF, know that I have an

opposite number in some unspecified Asian nation, whom I temporarily designate The Enemy. He knows everything about the Master Plan, as indeed I know everything about his similar work. We know that we know, and so forth.

'He is faceless to me, this General X, but I do know that his thoughts, plans, aspirations are much on the order of my own. He knows little of my movements, nor I of his, yet we can make necessary assumptions about one another which turn out to be correct. If they were not, our faulty logic would one day become explicit on the battlefield.

'Now I wish to subsume his thinking into the Master Plan. To do so, I must affect his system, drawing his soul into a snare while maintaining the integrity of my own soul. The fact our nations are at a stalemate underscores our equivalence; he is equally interested in entrapping my soul, or system. We make our secret plans and attack.)

'I am not a monster, forgive me, only a lesser card. The face cards you know only too well; the Communist bosses of Wall Street and Washington, the Fascist pigs of Moscow and Peking. I am a friend. I wanted only to live my life, solve my little calculus of war, and die. A decent burial with a free flag from the Veterans' Administration, that's all I wanted.

'Excuse me, I am of course terrifying; the face of death in the halls of *Life*. You are here to preserve my skin: I am here to take yours. Fair enough?

'Forgive me for being obscene pig. I have not the garment your race require for decent civilized discourse. Ignorant bastard, me. Have not even Jesus-boy laplap. Sorry, boss.

'Gentlemen, my work is *crucial* to the war effort. It is absolutely essential that I be left undisturbed, *not bled daily*, and so forth. I would like to see my aide, Captain Savage, as soon as he comes in. I am our only real guarantee of liberty – I do not exaggerate. I would like the bombing to stop between ten and twenty hundred hours, if you please. And for God's sake, take that burned child away to some other ward!'

The nurses are frozen, like the men in his dream. The throat of Dr Godden smiles at them from the floor.

'And the toilets are a disgrace. In conclusion, may I say that this has been a most successful year, fellows. I really mean it. The Enemy is everywhere, in our food and air, up our rectums and down our throats. But we have every confidence of an early victory. If we have to poison our food, burn our air, and flush our guts, I can promise you one thing – The Enema is finished! We will mop up his cells wherever we find them, and you have my word – the boys will be home for Christmas!' (*and standard purées. The only enjoyment left him at mealtime now was imagining the dietician ladling goop from tiny jars whose labels exhibited pretty babies. His hair began falling faster now, and there were sudden blinding headaches and spells of high fever. He was enveloped by a very ancient and fish-like smell which reminded him, when he happened to notice it, of woman.*

(4. J: an attractive first piece
 a. on earth
 b. in winter
 c. female dominant position
 d. conclusions
 (1) lazy and reluctantly responsive
 (2) engages only to be sociable
5. J: a nice tight second
 a. darkly tanned
 b. athletic socks
 c. boring
6. one night stand
7. not applicable
8. n/a
9. M: a rich third
 a. needed to get drunk for it
 b. eventually, so did I
10. O.n.s.
11. O.n.s.
12. S: a beautiful fourth
 a. almond eyes
 (1) ophidian eyes

(2) parenthetical
(A) made me think of parenthood
(B) made me wonder about her other, multiple parentheses

13. O.n.s.
14. R: a seductive fifth
a. passionate
b. intelligent
c. well-made
d. but
(1) error
(2) stillborn son changed things
e. suicide
(1) I made her nervous and sleepless
(2) the doctors gave her pills to make her sleep
(3) she slept
(4) with the TV on
(A) I thought she was watching the Big Picture
(B) Battle of the Bulge
(C) I watched it through, not knowing
(D) then called the doctor
(E) but she was dead when I got there
(F) really
f. parenthesis closed
g. all she wrote
15. Suggested designation: MIL-W-84007/3)

'I chose to destroy him with heart disease; he chose cancer for me. Thus far it seemed a stalemate again; each of us is drawn off against a new enemy, part of our energy and cognitive ability is thus diverted, and the significant changes in national strategic policy could now be examined.

'But The Enemy loses! Though he has established a salient within my brain, my REAL soul is intact. He is at my back, but my back is protected. He is at my window, behind me at the mirror when I shave, within my blood and soul – yet it is my soul which will subsume him entirely!'

The Master Plan has been given the above 'tall tale' and queried as to the nature of The Enemy. We are now awaiting significant results.

(Seven divisions wiped out on paper! He leaned against the bar, sick with defeat. The other junior officers at the NATO mess tactfully avoided his eye. Those who had seen the printout and the plotting board grinned, or seemed to grin.

He had forgotten that Leap Year gives February 29 days. It was that simple: him sitting helplessly watching the plotting board, while a clerk erased his seven immobilized divisions: The Enemy leapt on Leap Day.

(His teeth were on fire. He ran down the streets of Avalon laughing with pain. They began to pull the burning roots, and as his jaw came crumbling away, they drew him into the Avalon Theater.

The movie was in special code. He put on the strange cardboard glasses everyone else wore and these made him invisible. 'Gentlemen, Ruth is like the seven seas. I will translate her for you right now, if you please: Earth on earth, dust to dust. Get it?' Her cornsilk hair rattled across his face where it was burned.)

The razor blade cut through the silk-threads of the balsa sheet and skipped into his finger and out again. The blood was the colour of dirty bricks. He watched it drip down on the razor-nicked edge of the table. (watched the water-jug fling out a bouquet of water that hung there, shimmering. The movie was stuck or something; he got out of bed and went into the hall.

In the barracks, he found them frozen as the dawn had taken them, in a grotesque game of 'Statue'. One airman field-stripping a cigarette had just exposed the wet tobacco wound. Another, in the middle of shining one shoe, had tilted it to get the morning light.

The light continued, for the sun was stopped just above the horizon – with motes frozen in the stationary beams – to permit The Enemy an extra day of battle. The

General screamed out at them as the grindstone began to sing. And the God who stopped the sun over Gibeon was our own ¡po⅁ The map—

The map showed the cancer clearly, and Captain Savage walked a pair of dividers across it. 'The Ruth,' he explained, 'is right here.' The Avalon parents association was meeting to discuss what to do about the burned boy. 'He's blocking up Courthouse Square!' 'Yes, and that hideous "face" – or whatever you call it.'

The briefing was over, and he was up into the cockpit, off on Mission Ruth. Even on a contour map, he thought, her body was beautiful ... the lines enfolding it like parentheses)

That last night – if it were the last – he allowed Miss Nylon to turn on the TV. It began as a family comedy, and he dozed (the albino butcher). *The room was dark when he woke, and Miss Nylon was nearer. Machine-guns clattered in the corridor. No, in the flickering window. 'It's about Guadalcanal.' There was a strange look in Miss Nylon's eyes. 'If you like I can trim it off ...'*

'No, it's all right.'

'Al! I'm hit, Al!'

Takatakataka. 'This is it, kid!'

'You've certainly been grouchy, today. Is the pain ... ?'

'Al, I can't make it! Better – unh! – better go on without me. Leave me here.'

'Old Grouchy. Why, you haven't even made a pass today, you old goat.' Her eyes were glazed in death. She came nearer. She stood by the bed.

'Leave me here, I can hold 'em off. That's an order, soldier!'

'You old, oversexed goat.'

The rain outside was machine-gunning on the wide window. She turned to draw the curtain, and he saw the glitter of wet red lower lip.

'Hey Joe! Hey Yankee pig! I coming cut your throat plitty soon now!'

Takataka.

'*Sweet old grouchy goat.*') He is simply Old Grouchy to them now, the fear is over. Every once in awhile there comes a mad bull to the slaughterhouse – routine. Give him the usual sedative, drag him back to the numbered room, slip him between the mitred sheets. The day he dies they will cover him with the same sheet. Then they will walk down to the clean cafeteria, and eat meat and gravy, mashed potatoes with a dab of butter, and frozen peas. Miss Nylon will leave her potatoes, and Al the intern will tell her she needn't worry about her figure, it looks just fine . . .

(*Pretty Miss Nylon was taking off her white nylon uniform. The Zero came in low over the beach, probing for them with tines of fire budda-budda-budda.*

'*Sweet.*'

'*Christ!*'

(End of report.

(*something tells me I've been here before*

(*'Hi-yo, Silver! Away!'*

(all she wrote

(The albino butcher stood there, waiting, silent. White hair and skin, white apron and shirt, white hands holding the cleaver against the grindstone. Inscrutable in his white Oriental mourning. Unfathomable.

Chunk! 'Full fathom five my finger lies . . .'

Chunk! It didn't hurt at all! 'My face!'

(Within the dreamwork, a map of Littleworld is being plotted. The General leans over it, easing wind from a good dinner. His cigar taste accents the lingering flavour of the port.

Now he can see into it, the roofless hospital room, as a tiny Savage leans forward, ferret-eager over the dying feast.

'I begin to have bloody thoughts. The blood is leaking in my brain. I am changing into something rich and strange. This is all so real the General cannot help holding his cigar well away, lest he drop ash on the tiny figures,' says the doll in bed. 'My marriage has failed,

and now my health. It would be pleasant, very pleasant . . .'

'Absolutely senseless at the last,' says little Savage to little Dr Godden. 'It's a great pity. I ought really to destroy his final ruminations, to protect his reputation. But – well, regulations.'

Smiling, the General muses that tiny Savage has his own miniature cancer. He, Cancer, has won. He finishes the inert replica's sentence:

'. . . to imagine that The Enemy destroyed Ruth and fed cancer to my brain. But ultimately, the responsibility is *mine*.'

The face of the doll has become the color of the fine ash on his Extramaduro.)

Chunk! 'The dying man pays all debts . . . this is three . . .'

The five senses leave him by five wounds. A solid fifth, sweet numbness of the razor-nicked wooden block.

And it is Ruth who takes his carcass over her shoulder and carries him down to the snowy freezer. His cloven stomach enfolds her; he covers her again. . . .)

Anticipating his command, slime is drooling down his leg, as he drops the knife. And this is) **IT!**

Author's Note.

This story is told in nine parenthetical 'layers':

1. **The general's last word.**
2. A present tense account of the 'Battle of the Corridor' as he perceives it.
3. *A past tense account of the past few days in the hospital.*
4. **A medico-military report on 'the subject's' life, career and emotional state.**
5. *His top-secret monograph on The Master Plan.*

6. *Brief extracts from scenes of his childhood, youth and young manhood.*
7. An 'Item Description' of Woman as he sees her.
8. His dreams.
9. **A sub-dream 'reality' which permits him an overview of all of the above.**

Flatland

Dave and George sat in their cell playing checkers. The rough sunlight shone in through bars, illuminating their striped uniforms, the checkerboard, the ranks of parallel scratches on the wall that made a Crusoe calendar.

'My wife sent me this cake,' said George. 'Want some?'

'Why not?'

Clanking the chain that bound his ankle to a large cast-iron ball, George moved to the table. He began cutting the cake, then stopped. His fingers probed, crumbling.

'Hey, look!'

George held up a crumb-flecked hacksaw blade.

Bill read the paper at breakfast, while Mary, who had arranged her hair in curlers, poured coffee. She was opposed to capital punishment, though not unconditionally. She could not easily oppose, for example, putting to death as painlessly and humanely as possible, people who are shown to be *absolute murderers*, whose murderousness is invincible.

The question continued to occupy her long after Bill had run for his bus, until a vacuum cleaner salesman, braving the BEWARE THE DOG sign, rang the bell. While he demonstrated an inferior machine, Mary asked if he believed in capital punishment.

'I think it all depends,' he said, sprinkling dirt on the carpet. 'You could say that we're begging the question already, in even calling it "punishment". I think we should be perfectly aware of our own motives. Do we mean it to be a kind of euthanasia, do we mean it "to encourage the others", or is it to be just simple vengeance?' He left without finishing the cleaning operation. Mary meant to ask the postman, but this time Fido showed his advertised ferocity, driving him away.

Trixi and Mitzi, two chorus cuties, sat before their dressing-table mirrors discussing, as usual, men. Mitzi felt that men owed much of their character to operant conditioning, a technique that worked best on rodents. She pointed out men who fawned, panted, retrieved, shook hands and wet themselves, on command. Trixi, on the other hand, felt that free will and heredity, which she referred to as racial will-to-become, were major factors, conditioning only a novel side-effect of will-to-learn. The great herd of men were, she explained, simply built upon shifting genetic sands.

'You must meet Horace,' Mitzi said. 'He's a funny little bald man with a big white moustache. But he's rich.'

'That sounds like Major X!'

'Call me Hector, my dear,' said the major, sweeping off his silk hat as he came in. He presented Trixi with a dozen long-stemmed roses (one is pressed in her Self-Book still) and a diamond-encrusted manacle.

Mary and Barbara drove into the city to do a little shopping. The roads seemed crowded, and Mary noticed that most of the other drivers were women. They drove badly, making mainly mistakes of indecision, as though the whole region had been buried in existentialist snow. Mary had vivid memories of putting accordion pleats in the car's fender herself, against the garage door. She'd been afraid to confess to Bill.

When the two chums had finished their shopping, they took in a movie and then had tea at a Gypsy Tea Toom. Just for fun, Mary had her fortune told by an old woman with gold earrings. Gazing into her crystal ball, the old woman muttered that the fate of the world was of course uncertain, but not impossible. With judicious population controls, agricultural improvements, and large-scale planning along recycling lines, the balance might yet be tipped in a positive direction. She advised Mary to have no more children, to eat less meat, to collect paper and scrap metals, and not to flush her toilet quite so often.

Driving home, Mary and Barbara were struck by how many motorcycle police were hidden behind billboards.

Bill seemed slightly shocked by the price Mary'd paid for her new hat. 'I guess it's due to the old wage–price inflation spiral, though,' he said, lifting his feet for her passing with the vacuum cleaner. She swept away the last of the odious salesman's dirt, and the price tag of her hat.

Walter and Dave stood meditating upon the sales graph on the office wall. It showed a clearly declining jagged line. The Acme Vacuum Cleaner Company was entering, as Dave put it, a dark night of the soul. The question remained whether it would emerge purified and purged of its baser nature, and fit to serve its creator.

'Shall we go see Mr Gordon?'

Walter shrugged. 'Why bother? He'll only be sitting there with his blonde secretary Doreen on his lap, "dictating".'

Walter was wrong. At that moment, Doreen and Mr Gordon sat in separate chairs, to which they had been bound. Mr Gordon was trying to work his gag loose enough to use the telephone. Doreen could only stare horrified at the empty shallowness of the modern office safe, which stood open.

Not a week later, Mitzi was implicated in a serious crime. The judge was on her side – so much could be inferred from the way he leaned over the bench to watch her cross her legs – but the jury needed more persuading. Luckily she could count upon Major X to provide a well-known and eloquent lawyer, Bill Grass.

Summing up for the defense, Bill explained that, just as the Copernican revolution had discplaced man from the center of the universe, just as the Darwinian revolution displaced man from his privileged position in the Great Chain of Being, so too had the Einsteinian revolution destroyed man's last assurances that size, duration and speed were real, absolute values. Bill showed how, cut loose from faith and tradition, adrift in modern anomie, Mitzi had faltered. As they moved to acquit her, many of the jury were not ashamed to weep.

Dr Penn, wearing his white jacket and speculum, explained to Hector Gordon just what a heart attack was. Mr Gordon scarcely listened. At length he interrupted:

'Listen, doctor, the important thing is, life has become intensely *real*. The most ordinary objects have taken on a gloss of newness, a translucency of gem mystery. For the first time, I see what the business of life really is. That speculum of yours might be a monocle, for example. The stethoscope in your hand might be a glass of pink gin. Yes, and the eye chart on the wall behind you might be a wall of trophy animal heads, arranged in order of size, beginning with the great E elephant . . .'

That weekend began with Al Cullenor, the new neighbor, borrowing the lawn mower. Bill and Mary decided to take the kids to the beach. On the way, they discussed sex education quite freely in front of the children, by using a form of 'pig latin' Bill had learned at Law School. 'Aturobnay ovidesobpray omanobway ithobway a uilt-inobay atorobindicay of the imeobtay eobshay is ulatingobovay, onsistingobcay of ightobslay ampsobcray ompaniedobaccay by a inobthay aginalobvay ecretionobsay faintly colored with oodobblay,' Bill opined. 'German scientists long ago learned to call this phenomenon *Mittelschmerz*,' Bill opined.

They were lost, driving in the wrong direction.

Major X knew there must be more to life than standing here in his trophy room, drinking pink gin. Somehow the elephant and the rhino had lost their freshness; looking at the musk ox, he no longer felt the crisp thrill born when his charge slammed home . . .

'The city, too, has its wild pulse of jungle noises,' he told himself, 'its secret struggles, its heart of dankness.'

He went out into it, strolling in the noonday sun without his helmet. High on a girder, he could see steelworkers eating lunch.

Al Cullenor straddled a girder and opened his lunch box. What he found there was so shocking that . . .

Major X passed on into the park. He passed ragged George, asleep under a copy of the *Wall Street Journal*, and he passed the bench where N. Decting was proposing to Lida Norse. The Major found a bench of his own. It was not until he rose from it that he realized it was freshly painted: His coat was tigered.

'Marked!' he cried, and fled. Past a blind beggar selling pencils. Past a bearded prophet whose sign advised him to Repent. Past a street vendor selling tiny wind-up dolls. On into a department store, to the Complaint Department.

On his way home, the Major stopped to watch a fire. A fireman made his way down a ladder, carrying a blonde named Darlene.

They finally admitted they were lost and asked directions of a rustic in bib overalls. Leaning over a rail fence and chewing a blade of grass, he explained to them that in the ultimate sense, all directions were one. Bill and Mary Grass drove on into the desert, past the bleached skulls of cattle. A few miles from the road, though they did not know it, George was crawling in the sand, dying of thirst.

Now and then Pa and Ma Norse looked into the living room to watch the young couple on the sofa. It was in much the same spirit that Dave had looked in, one day, on the waiting room of the patent office. A dozen men sat waiting, each holding a package of unusual shape on his lap. To Barbara, it was much the same as the other waiting room, in which Dave had waited until the nurse told him it was triplets. It was in that very hospital that Al lay recovering from his twenty-story fall: a mass of bandages, with all four limbs held up in traction splints, to an elaborate arrangement of wires, pulleys and weights. Thus gravity would cure, he reflected, what it had caused.

Walter had a table alone, in a corner of the hotel restaurant near a placard: WATCH YOUR HAT AND COAT. There was an unusual object in his soup, and Walter called the waiter's attention to it.

The stag dinner for N. Decting was being held in another room at the hotel. Out of an immense cake leapt Trixi, who often danced on the tables until dawn. Bill was embarrassed. Any nakedness reminded him of the human condition, of answering the telephone wrapped in a bath towel.

On the beach, Bill sneaked a look at a pair of bikini blondes named Doreen and Darlene, while Mary sneaked a look at him. Finally he dozed, dreaming of dramatic news headlines like:

> WORLD DECLARED A MARXIST PARADISE, themselves being expanded into great boxwood word blocks that were being shoved forward to chock up the sagging floor of sand.

Meanwhile the kids buried Bill in sand.

On the drive home, Bill and Mary sat in front, while the kids slept dreamlessly in the back seat. Bill pointed out to Mary that a flying saucer had landed in the desert, and that a short green man could be seen making his way from it towards a telephone booth.

Mr Gordon found he couldn't sleep, partly because he'd taken a nap in the afternoon, producing Zs. Now he tried counting sheep, visualizing them leaping one by one over a rail fence . . . into what?

A strange noise. Mr Gordon crept downstairs and looked into the dining room. The man who was putting silver into a satchel wore a flat cap, a black eyemask, and a jacket over a striped sweater. He worked by flashlight.

'Asia,' said the burglar, turning his beam upon Mr Gordon, 'is the key. As Japan begins to play an increasing role in shaping the economic future of the world, China may shake off her mantle of mystery and challenge the island giant to open industrial warfare. In any case, we must watch Asia, the world's weathercock.'

The Dectings' honeymoon took them to Asia, to a place not far from where Major X had hunted the tiger from a howda. In the marketplace, the Dectings saw snake charmers, fakirs, reclining on beds of nails, and the famous Indian Rope Trick.

Major X and Trixi were sitting in water up to their necks in a large cast-iron pot. This had been set to boil on an open fire, while black men danced around them, brandishing spears. The black men all wore grass skirts and bones through their noses.

'I wish I knew the reason,' said the Major earnestly. 'I really wish I'd studied a bit of anthropology, instead of all that blasted art history.' Then, there being some time to kill before they boiled, he explained to Trixi the cloud-formulae which Constable seemed to have learned from Alexander Cozens.

George was at last a prisoner again. This time he was manacled to the wall, hanging by his wrists. Nearby hung a stranger in the same plight.

'There is a game called Prisoner's Dilemma,' George said. 'We assume that two men have been caught by the police and are questioned separately. Each can either talk or keep quiet. If one confesses, he'll get ten years, and his companion will be executed. But if both confess, they'll both get life imprisonment. Finally, if neither confesses, they'll both be freed.

'According to the rule of game theory, each man should confess. But common sense tells us they can do better by both keeping quiet. It's quite a puzzle.'

The other did not reply. At dawn, George was taken outside, stood against a wall and shot. As he died, the ground beneath him seemed to go translucent, like the smoke of the cigarette he had just refused. George could almost make out words beneath the world.

Finally Dave was cast up on a desert island. Though only a few yards in diameter, it featured a single palm tree against which he could rest, while he waited.

A Game of Jump*

Bill was in love with another woman, so he put an end to Clara, and to their two children, Dot and Eddie. Eddie had on a blue cap at the time and Dot had her doll with the red hair. Bill did not like to do this to them, but he had to. Dot and Eddie saw him do it to Clara, and there was nothing Bill could do about that, then.

Bill put the blue cap on the back seat of his car, and he would not let Ann, the other woman, take it out. There was no way for Ann to ask him if the police would find out about this, and if she did ask him, Bill would only say no. Ann said nothing.

They went to the farm, where Ann saw a black horse and a white cow. When she saw a pig, she said, I saw a pig make it with another pig once, and it was not very nice. I don't like pigs. Could I have some milk?

Bill went to ask the farm man for a cup of milk. When he had left her on her own, Ann said, I know, he did not do this thing for me. Nothing is any good any more.

Here is your milk, said Bill, all at once right next to her. What was it you said just now?

Nothing, dear. I wish we could go away to some other place, some new place, where we have never been before.

We can, we can. Only I have to be back at work in a day or two. The man I work for would not like it if I went away for a long time.

* Written with a 307-word vocabulary (the 300 Key Words listed in *A Second Ladybird Key Words Picture Dictionary and Spelling Book* by J. McNally (Wills & Hepworth, Loughborough, 1966), and seven proper nouns.

They got back into the car and went to Ann's place. A man from the police was by the door. Did you see a little boy? he asked. With a round head?

No, said Bill, we did not. If we do, we will let you know.

Do that, said the man, who was black. Do just that. Tell the police at once.

We will, we will.

Bill and Ann went into the house. Ann made them a drink, and then they went to bed.

On the bus, Felix said to the woman he was sitting just back of, Do you see this?

Yes, said Granada. She did not look so old in black.

This is no toy. It don't use caps. It says danger. I want you to get off the bus when I do, and don't try any games. Come with me.

Are you with the police?

All of us are with the police, these days. Just do what I tell you, or it will be the end.

Do you want me, is that it? All right, get it over with, she said.

Nothing like that. I want to talk to you, that is all. You do what I say, now.

It was all a game of jump, said Bill. I was in this new road, where all the men and every woman was new. I went to eat a rabbit egg, and all at once, it was a big, big apple cap. My lost love would call out to me from the window of the police station, but I had to learn how to get in to her.

Then Daddy was at the window of the three o'clock train, saying danger, danger. The train fell from a new tree, and I saw it was Dot, my Dot. She was my father, my train, see? That year the letters were big as dinner box picture, and today the wish woman came three times to ask my toy bus a Christmas day. It was only a baby now, and the door would not open. I did open the book of Ask-Me, and then I had to learn which

Mummy to sing the time name thing to. All at once I went up, up, up.

So you think, said Ann. We can get up now.

They got out of bed and went out to buy a new car. It was green, and the old one was blue. They went to a cafe.

The thing is, Bill said, when they had sat down at a table by the window, many men do these things, and no one thinks a thing about it. I don't talk of Clara and the children, but many a man, many a man had made his life over in one way or another. The sun is very hot at this table.

It is always very hot, she said. Tell me, do you love me?

More tea? said Bill. Or how about some apple jam?

I feel like an egg.

So do I. I am an egg, a rabbit egg, found under a tree.

Stop. This is not the time or the place for that, said Ann. Back to my place? This street always says danger to me. We should go away.

I think we had best go back to my place, said Bill. I forgot about the dog. He may eat Clara.

They went back to his house, and Bill put an end to Felix, his black and white dog. Ann did not look too well, so they went for a nice drink then.

You look good in red, said Bill.

Thanks.

Do you make much money? asked Granada. Buy me a drink.

I do make very much money, but I have no money at all right now, Felix said. Let me tell you about my work, and we will walk over to my place. The first house on that next street.

What a nice street, she said. Trees and flowers and all just like a picture. And right next to the police station. How very nice. I would like to live here.

You do live here, he said. You are Mrs Felix, but you don't know it any more.

Is that right? she said. Have I lost my – you know?

Right. On days, I work at the train station, making the trees look good. On other days, I work right over there at the fire station, that one. I make toys for children who have none, like the Bill children. For Christmas.

And what do you do for fun. This?

No, for fun I go to the school and give all the little boys and girls sweets. Then I take them home with me and do bad things with them.

At the door, he said, I have had some fun with you, too.

What?

It is only a toy one, after all. See, it has water in it.

But it was not a toy, as they then found out.

There was a fly in the house where Clara and Dot and Eddie and the dog Felix were. It went from Clara to Dot, from Dot to Felix, from Felix to Eddie, from Eddie to Clara, from Clara to Felix, from Felix to Dot, from Dot to Eddie, from Eddie to Felix, from Felix to Clara, from Clara to Eddie from Eddie to Dot, and from Dot to Clara. Then it made a stop on the cake on the dinner table.

Is that the car that had the boy's green cap? asked one man from the police.

Blue cap, said the other. It is the one, all right.

Blue, was it? Or green?

Blue I think. Yes, blue. That is Mr Bill's car. He works with pencils, they say. Let us take a look.

At the car or the cap?

At the car, which is green, and the cap, which is blue.

Why is that, do you think?

I wish I could fly just like a bird, said Ann. Don't you?

Not like. As a bird. No I don't wish for a thing, thanks. I have a very good time, Bill said. I like this drink.

But I could fly away to the sea, and play in the sun, and do so many fun things. In the water, too.

Those things are not so much fun when you get to do them, Bill said, after all. I did want to be a rabbit egg, but not any more. I think I will see if that girl over there would like a drink.

My name is Bill, he said to the girl. Who are you?
Dot, she said. May I take your picture?

I don't get it, said one police man. This cap was green before, and now it is blue. Do you think some little boy, like the little boy who is wanted, could take the green one away and put a blue one in its place?

I just don't know. Why don't we call the station and see?

Granada was not very well. She was on the table and Felix was about to help her get well. Think of a train station or a horse farm, he said. Then it will not be so bad. Tell me, do you know where you are, and who?

I know that when I was a little girl I had a big doll, in the afternoon.

I don't get that. In the afternoon when you were a little girl?

I could only play with it in the afternoon, that is to say. The name of this doll was Clara. And I had a dog named Felix, who came only when you did not call him, and many, many books. The best were *How to Make Money at Home* and *Birds that Sing*.

This will not get us any place, said Felix. How about me, and our four children: Bill, Clara, Dot and Eddie?

Nothing. Nothing at all, she said.

You are no fun to be with, then. I would never take you to the sea or any other place, Felix said.

The sea? I wish I could fly just like a bird, don't you? And I would fly away to the sea, and play in the sun, and do many fun things. In the water too – I know, my name is Ann.

Where is Ann? said Bill. He looked for her under the table and chairs. Then he asked a big, round man if he saw her go out.

The woman in red? She was here just now, said the man. I did not see her go.

I just went over to talk to the picture girl, and when I came back, she had left.

Women, said the big, round man. We can not live with them,

and we can not live with out them. We live and learn, don't we?

Now we know Bill had an old blue car as well as his new green one, said the black man from the police. The other police man said little. They were at the station, where they had just had a talk with some other police men.

And we know Bill has a little boy like the boy we want. I think I see how this goes. Let us make a call on Bill, what do you say?

Another police man said, but we found the green cap in a tree by the train station. I think another boy went on the train but you may be right, at that.

When is a door not a door? asked Bill. He was slow in the head, from all that drink, and very red.

I don't know, said the big, round man. Tell me.

When it is a jam.

Very good. Have another, on me. Now stop me if you know this one . . .

Say, said a little boat man who came in just then, the police have your car, Bill.

My car? asked Bill. The green one?

Yes. They went off over the hill in it, to the police station. My, you don't look too well.

They went to my house, said Bill, going white.

Yes, but stop me if you know this one, said the big man. Two pigs made it in a well, see, and this other cat came by and saw them at it, and—

Two police men were going over Bill's house. Is that an egg over there? asked one.

No, it is the boy's ball. And that is the little girl's doll. I don't like the look of this at all. Why would any good woman do this, to her and her children?

And her dog, said the other. She must have been – you know. Here, have some of this cake. Very good, and it would just go bad if we did not eat it now. Go on.

Thanks. I would just like to know what the green cap has to do with all this, said the first. He looked at Clara and Eddie and Felix (or what was left of them) under the table. I would just like to know where the little girl is. And how could this little boy here take the green cap and put the blue one in its place?

I don't feel so well, said the other. I think there must have been a fly in this cake.

You did not do what you said to those school children, Ann said to Felix.

No, he said, I did not. By the way, where did you get that red thing from? I like you in red.

You made fun of me.

'Yes – I like children. I have a little boy here, in a box. He has a green cap on his head. Would you like to have a look at him?

Why is he in a box?

Felix said, well, I found him taking some fish from my dinner table. So I put him this box and closed it up, to make him learn what is best and what is not. That is not so bad of me, is it? Am I so bad?

Not at all, said Ann, but let him out now.

I will. Just let me get this open.

But there was no one in the big box.

He got away! How do you like that? He got away with my cake.

Your cake? Was it not your fish?

Fish cake, it was. But he will not want to do that again, I think. Say, do you know any more about who you are?

Yes, said Ann. I once came to a door that said PUSH and gave it a pull, and it came open. And if I want to write a letter, I will use milk for ink, so then the boy or girl who gets it can take it to a fire and let it get hot and there will be the letter. Today I had a drink of milk at the farm.

I give up, said Felix. Let us take a bus to the bus station, where I will put you on your right bus.

I could write a book, said Bill, about all I have said and should not have said. Where is that woman? She is no more, like the flowers of last year.

Time is going fast, said the big, round man. They say you cannot put your hand into the same water two times. Because it is going too fast. He did sing:

If I were only white
Then I could write
To bring this top
To a stop
If I were only green
I would tell the Queen
To take the train
When you see rain
But I am black and blue. So blue.

This man was red, and so was Bill, from the drink.

But she made the dinner I like best, said Bill. Fish cake. I don't know where she could have got the fish from, at this time of year.

We are all fish, said the old boat man. We live in an Ask Me book. Our love is a fish love, and our every wish—

Not me, said Bill. I am a rabbit. And the only book I read is *How to Make Money at Home.*

The two police men were not well. It must have been the cake, said one, and fell down.

But the cap. The green cap is just right for this boy's head, said the other, and fell down next to him.

At three o'clock the other police found them all: the woman Clara, the dog Felix, and the two police men. They must have been right about that boy in the green cap, said one. Another said, this is what they do to those who know too much. We had best put out a call right now for the little girl.

I did it, I did it, said Bill. Clara and the children yes and the dog too. Why did I do it?

Money? asked the big, round man.

Felix looked out the window of the bus at the danger. Why will men in green cars do that? he said. There is room for him and for the bus, but that man wants all the street for his own.

Ann did not look out, and said nothing. She read a book.

You have had too much to drink, said the big man. I cannot give you any more. Do I have to draw you a picture? Go home.

I wish I could, said Bill. I only wish I could. Give me another, will you?

No. Not if you was my brother. Go to bed.

But I have no car, no children, nothing, said Bill, going red.

If I were a dog, said Felix, I would go after that car and get it. I would.

Ann read: We are all fish. She closed the book.

I was down by the train station today, she said. With a blue cap on my head. I went up in a tree to look at the big train.

I am a dog, said Felix. As the bus came to a stop, he jumped down and ran after the green car. Night was upon them.

Night fell.

We have the green car, so it must be that blue cap we are now after, said one of the police men. If we can only get to the train station in time, we can stop that girl, before she gets another man or woman.

You talk like a man who eats fish cake, said another. It is the *green* cap we want, and it is at the *bus* station. The cap is upon a *boy*, one who got it at the fire station. Here, you can not run this car well. Let me have a go at it.

Let go! Look out! That dog! That bus!

There is my car, said Bill. He ran into the street. Look out for the bus! said the big, round man.

Two queens sat just back of Ann on the bus. Did we run over a rabbit, dear? asked the one called Dot.

That is his bag, said the other, who had the name Clara. Tell me, sweets, can I keep this green cap?

That old thing? Blue is it not? Yes, do keep it. I found it today under a tree. By the station. It is just right for your head, you know?

The Hammer of Evil
or
Career Opportunities at the Pascal Business School

Through the barred window, a blue Magritte sky. I've told them, I'm as innocent as any angel that ever danced on the head of any pin. They can't keep me.

'Getting out of here?' Professor Rice grins. 'Nothing easier. I can leave anytime I like.'

'I know, I know. It's all how you look at it. Professor, if you've said that once, you must have said it a thousand ti—'

The meter in the wall clicks, and a printed card slips out. It reads: *Surely you mean that, if he has said it a thousand times, he must have said it once. Otherwise explain.*

They, the Acamarians, are pretty hot on explanations. I throw the card on the heap in the corner. Some lucky prisoner has the makings of a card house. Not me, I'm ready for execution. When I tell them I have nothing to lose, they ask me to explain.

'If I close my eyes, the world goes. (All but the smell of my unwashed cellmate.) You can't kill me, or I'll take the world with me. You can destroy my soul, but my body will go marching on.' That usually impresses them, especially when I march around the cell with my eyes shut.

When that fails, I can always tell them that past and future are all the same to me.

The cell door clangs open theatrically. A new man is thrown in. I am wary, for two reasons: (a) His ugliness. The yellow teeth, blackheads in ears, greased-down black hair with white dandruff, fat neck with boils – could he be an agent, trying for sympathy? (b) Anyway, he smells. Could be a way of breaking me down. They don't know the secret resources of Yuri Trumbull, though.

'Hello. They got you, too?'

I nod. Nods are safe, they give them information only one bit at a time. An old trick I learned from an Apache programmer. Trumbull is wily. My companion offers his hand. Scabs.

'Don't you know me?' he says. 'I know I'm not at my best, but—'

'Professor Rice!' I haven't seen him for, what, fifteen years. Professor Rice, of the good old Pascal Business School. 'What a coincidence!' More of their work, I'm thinking. But I know all about coincidences. I'm an actuary. Professor Rice is an antiquary. The Acamarians caught him in the Antarctic, digging up – why am I telling all these silly lies?

'So they got you, too,' he says again. 'My star pupil.' He sits on his bunk, marking territory with a noisy fart. 'Where was it?'

I begin inventing the past, as it really was. 'At work. I had just calculated the life expectancies for a Mormon waiter whose mother owns her own rhubarb, and a bricklayer who races his catamaran. The Mormon lives longer.'

'Fascinating. How much longer?'

Yuri Trumbull isn't saying. Wouldn't they just like to get their tentacles (or claws or whatever they have) on that vital piece of inside information!

'I finished, and my pocket calculator read 808,327,338. Bob Deal, at the next desk, started rambling on about probabilities. "I've got six reports here," he said, "from different places. Six people who took out life insurance, effective midnight, June the sixth. One minute later, each of them was killed by lightning. Incredible."

' "I believe it," I said.

'Bob has a short temper, it has something to do with his wooden neck. "Listen, it's about as likely as all the air in this room rushing over to one side and leaving a vacuum. Not impossible, but not bloody likely, either. There's devilry in it."

'I looked at my pocket calculator upside down. It read BEELZEBOB. "Hey Bob, here's a funny coincidence for you!"

'He didn't answer. All the air had rushed away from his part of the room, leaving a vacuum. Well, I took the hint. Ever since, I've been a devout—'

'Mormon?'

'No, bricklayer. It's the sincerest form of prayer, according to my wife.'

Professor Rice blew his nose and looked at his handkerchief thoughtfully, like a customer at the hors d'oeuvres table. 'I didn't know you were married.'

'My prayers have not been answered, no. But who knows? A few more bricks . . . As he suffocated, Bob wrote down the combination to the wall safe on his blotter. I opened the wall safe and looked through it to a blue Magritte sky. Blue, I tell you!'

He offered me a sandwich. Staring at his black fingernails, I declined.

'Taking a light carbine from the office wall, I crawled into the safe and on through. Magritte country, all right. A lot of men in bowler hats standing around, striking poses. I could fairly smell the green apples. This could only be London. The wind was from the south-southeast at a steady—'

'Get to the telegram part,' he said, spitting crumbs.

How did he know about that? Was he inventing my past?

'It was handed to me from a train window. It said, A CRUST OF BREAD IS BETTER THAN NOTHING. NOTHING IS BETTER THAN HEAVEN. So it was you who sent it?'

'I couldn't leave the train,' he protested. 'I was investigating a murder – or its opposite, really.'

I'll work that into my past somehow. I'm in the driver's seat again.

I first knew Professor Rice as a brisk, white-toothed young teacher, leading the Statistical Anomaly seminar. Very advanced stuff, for kids who only wanted to sell insurance.

'Trumbull, let's have that paper on the Prisoner's Dilemma.'

Game theory. Two men are captured by the enemy, and questioned separately. If, say, A confesses, and B doesn't, A will be freed, given a huge reward and treated as a hero. B will be shot. If both men confess, they'll serve life sentences at hard labor. If both keep their mouths shut, they'll be released. What should B do?

We have been questioned separately, the Professor and I. What did he tell them? That I was his star pupil? Or that he found the conclusions of my paper invalid?

'Professor Rice, have you actually seen them face-to-face?'

'Of course not, my boy.' The patronizing tone. 'No one has actually seen the Acamarians. That's partly how they keep their power. Talk about culture shock! Frankly, this invasion is getting on my nerves. No, we have to take their existence on faith. Oh, did I tell you I'm writing a novel about God?'

Years after our seminar, I met him on a tube train. He crosses London every day, to an office in the financial district. There he works on his long-awaited novel. Even then, I could see the signs of deterioration: The nap coming off his bowler, glasses taped together at the temple. He held a clipboard, and seemed to be counting the passengers. I invent the conversation:

'Hello, Professor. What's this?'

'Working over a theory, Trumbull. Counting the number of people who get on and off. At every station, more people get off the train than on. Curious, eh?'

'Every station? That's impossible.'

He made a face. 'Please. Never use that word. There are two perfectly plausible explanations. (a) People are being generated right inside this carriage, somehow. (b) The word "more" doesn't mean what it used to mean.'

I counted the passengers at the next station.

'Your theory's wrong. I just saw three people get into this carriage, and only one got out.'

'You didn't see the others, then? That *is* fascinating.'

Fascinating, his favorite word. He hisses it, sticking out the yellow lower teeth. He is fascinated by paradoxes, and by found bits of his own excessive body dirt.

A sad decline: Shiny bowler and hallucinations.

He yawns, exposing food, exhaling the smell of death. What could be more unlikely, in any universe, than being locked into a cell with this living corpse? Otherwise, it wouldn't be so bad: smooth grey stone walls, wooden bunks, not bad. The food could improve, especially the *pollo soppresso*. Rice prefers his packed lunches (where does he get them?), thin tomato-margarine sandwiches, he bites the dry crusts better than heaven, he throws the scraps on the floor.

'Do they let you smoke here?' He rolls a dirty little rag of a cigarette. 'Go on. You saw men in bowlers . . .'

'They rushed me, brandishing their umbrellas. How was I to know they were making for a train? I opened fire.'

'But it didn't work?'

'I see you know this country well, Professor. In order to reach the heart of a businessman dressed as Kafka, the bullet must first get halfway to him. Then it must go half the remaining distance, and so on, an infinite number of smaller and smaller steps. It's all too much for the bullet, so it gives up. Motion is impossible.'

'All things are possible with God,' he counters.

The next card asks him to elaborate.

'God can do anything. He could even cure poor old Zeno's dreams of impotence. I refer to Zeno the Greek philosopher, and not to Zeno the highly literate English prisoner.'

He received a THANK YOU card, the first I've seen.

'The bullet fell from the end of the gun and rolled around on the platform. One of the commuters tripped and fell down on it, and it lodged in his heart. So I'm here for a murder I didn't commit.'

'A likely story,' says Rice. He means it; his very boils are bursting with approbation. 'My own case is similar. I'm an antiquary, as you know. While digging in the Antarctic, I happened to find two rare old bronze coins. A Greek piece marked "51 B.C.", and a British coin marked "George I". These have proved fraudulent, and they say I planted them myself.

'They produced three witnesses who swear they saw me do it. I offered to produce thirty who would swear they didn't see me do it, but there: The guilty are always caught, you know.'

A card asks for explanation.

'If a man is guilty, he is always caught for his crimes. Another way of saying the same thing is, if a man is not caught, he's not guilty. We have only to look around and find a man who's never been caught. Is he innocent? Of course he is. There are millions of uncaught innocent men. Samuel Butler, to name but three.

'So I was caught.' He drops the ragged cigarette and digs a finger in his ear. 'The interrogation was odd. They asked me all about an old problem from the seminar.'

I'm not listening. Bread is better than heaven, is it? The lazy loaves drift quietly across our sky. Really they're Acamarian spacecraft, I suppose, powered by sheer nerve. Our nerve is gone, we're the suppressed chickens. I want out. I want the clean smell of fresh deodorant again. Is it true that, merely by using spray deodorants, humanity destroyed the Earth's ozone layer? And did that open the way to our invaders? I must look it all up in the prison library. Before dawn, and the firing squad.

'A prisoner is told by the governor that he'll be hanged one day in the coming week, but not on any day he's expecting it.' He's rambling again. 'Now he knows he can't be executed on Saturday. If they haven't killed him on any of the other six days, they can't kill him on the seventh, when he'll certainly be expecting it. So Saturday is out.'

Why do so many paradoxes involve prisoners and hanging?

'By the same reasoning, Friday is out. Since it has to be one of the six days, it can't be the sixth, because he must expect it by then. Friday is out, Thursday is out, and so on. He eliminates each day until he's left with only Sunday. But they can't hang him then, either, because he now expects it. So they can't hang him at all.'

The Acamarians aren't too bright. They really don't see the rest of it. Our prisoner reasons that they can't hang him on any day of the week, so he's never expecting it. So they can hang him anytime.

'They want answers,' says my cell-mate. 'Tell them nothing.'

The interrogation room is like the first-class compartment of a luxury flight. You scrunch down in your comfortable seat with your earphones. If they like your answers, they show you movies. I've seen both of their excellent, all-family selections: *Keys of the Kingdom* (Gregory Peck meets God) and *My Friend Flicka* (Roddy MacDowall meets horse).

Under intensive interrogation, and bribed with chicken and butter, I tell them about prisoners A, B and C.

'The governor tells them that two will hang, and one will be set free. A says to the governor, "Tell me the name of one of the other men who will hang. If both of them are going to be hanged, just tell me either name."

'The governor says, "B will hang."

'A now sees that his survival chances have increased. Earlier, he had one chance in three of surviving. Now, either C or himself will go free, so his chances are one in two.

' "Wait," says the governor. "Suppose I said C instead of B?"

' "My chances would still improve in the same way."

' "Suppose I said nothing at all, then."

' "It's still the same. You'd be suppressing one name or the other, and, no matter which, my chances would still be one in two." '

This baffles them. They can't see why the governor is in the story at all. A could simply imagine a governor coming to him and speaking a name. So A's chances of survival are always one in two?

'That's right,' I lie. Why do I enjoy lying to them? They're doing their best.

I finally ask Professor Rice to put his escape plan into action.

'All right. Look at the corner of the cell. There, see where the ceiling and floor corners are? Now, why do they have to be inside corners? Couldn't they just possibly be the outside corners of a crooked cube?'

I stare at them until they are. We jump back, avoiding the big lop-sided cube as it falls over. We're free.

Two other freed prisoners rush over to thank him. They even shake his hand.

'I'm A,' says the taller. 'This is my cell-mate, B. I'm afraid C was crushed beneath a big stone block. Good thing his insurance coverage started a few minutes ago.'

The four of us get on a train (and five get off). Professor Rice finds his clipboard on the floor and makes a note.

I feel I've heard A's story before: 'B and I are related. We hang around together, doing odd jobs. You know, chopping wood, pumping water in and out of tanks. Or racing. We race a lot. Rowboats, upstream and downstream, stuff like that. Good clean fun.'

What is it I like about A so much?

'Fun!' B has the shoulder slump of a born loser. 'Like if I ride a bike from X to Y, A has to race me in a car, passing me at—'

'That's not fair,' A says. 'You generally have twice as many apples as I do, before you give me half the—'

'Give, give, give! It's been the same ever since you were as many years old as I am younger than you were when—'

'Ignore him.' A turns to me. 'It all goes back to our parents, a lawyer and a model. They met at a footrace. The lawyer could go faster uphill and on the level, but mother was faster on the downhill parts. So naturally mother won.'

Professor Rice does not look up from his work. 'I take it you mean the lawyer was your mother.'

B, still sulking, says, 'A's not my brother, you know.'

I feel it's true.

'It's true!' Professor Rice is fascinated. 'I calculate the number of passengers generated within this carriage as exactly – uh, I have the figures here – exactly *one*.'

I hate to say it. 'Professor, have you counted yourself?'

He adjusts his taped glasses, turns over the pages on his clipboard for a moment or two. Finally he says:

'Have I told you about my novel?'

The train wheels begin to scream. I know what's happened: The tracks are getting narrower as we near the horizon.

I get off alone at the next station. (No one gets in.) Along the deserted platform, I hear voices from the exit tunnels. Going alone through the tunnel, I hear feet and voices on the escalators.

No one is on the escalators. No one in the ticket-collector's box, where I find his burning cigarette on the shelf. Outside there are traffic noises, murmuring mobs of shoppers, the cry of a newspaper man. But of course when I get there, it's to see: abandoned cars; a stack of papers peeling off and blowing away; an ice-cream cone on the pavement, just starting to melt. London, perhaps the world, is one big *Mary Celeste*, with everyone suddenly out to lunch.

Professor Rice's office is here, in a blue glass tower where brokers and lawyers, on a normal day, might sit and reason with one another.

All I can find of his novel is in the typewriter:

'If I'm God,' said God, who was, 'then why can't I do anything I like? Why can't I lock myself in a prison from which even I can't escape?'

He found this, like all questions, rhetorical.

'I know the answer to that one,' he cried, paring his fingernails. 'The answer is, even *I* can't contradict myself. Ha!'

Ha indeed. One crummy idea, in a half-dozen lines, and that cribbed from Aquinas. Nor any explanation of the fingernails. (Can the Infinite grow?) Why can't God contradict himself, anyway?

I look out over the blue city. At any moment, the alien invasion could begin. For centuries, the hordes of Acamar have been on the way: Levering themselves slowly through space; hand-over-hand (if they have hands) along weightless ropes, through frictionless pulleys, dragged along by perpetual motion . . .

When the first few loaves appear in the sky, I begin the incantation:

'A certain barber of Acamar shaves all the Acamarians who do not shave themselves. Does he shave himself?'

They think it over and mail a card to me: *Can there be such a barber?*

There can't. He twinkles out of existence.

Taking a deep breath, I say, 'If a barber does not exist, neither do his customers.'

No one on Acamar shaves himself. Already plumes of smoke trail from a few loaves, before sunset the fields will be full of warm toast: fodder for the gentle, lowing, purple beasts.

The Locked Room

Another Fenton Worth Mystery

Fenton Worth instructed his valet Bozo to turn away all callers for the rest of the evening.

'I mean to spend a quiet evening with a good book,' said the popular private detective, and indicated a new, calf-bound volume on the library table.

Bozo smirked, knowing what usually happened to all such 'quiet evenings' in the life of a famous sleuth. 'I imagine, sir,' he said, 'that a beautiful lady will burst in, begging you to save her life. That, or else Inspector Grogan will ask you to help recover the Stilton diamonds.'

The well-known private dick smiled. 'Not tonight, Bozo. I mean it: No calls of any kind. If it is a matter of life and death, as is usual, refer our caller to the police. Other cases I can look into in the morning. For now, I'm going to lock myself in the library, and I don't want to be disturbed.'

With that, the eminent criminologist shooed his servant from the room, turned the key and settled into his favorite Morris chair with the 'good book'. It was a detection novel, entitled *The Locked Room.*

'*The Locked Room*, eh? That should be of considerable interest,' he mused, toying with his letter opener. This curious instrument was actually a Moro weapon, an example of that knife with a wavy blade familiar to crossword buffs as a *kriis*. Opening the volume, Fenton used the *kriis* to slit a few pages, then began to read.

The plot of this novel, shorn of its ornaments, misdirections and other fanciful elements, was simple: A man was found dead in a sealed room, locked from the inside. No one else was found in the room, and though the death was certainly a homicide, no weapon could be found. Suspects were abundant, yet how could any of them have done it?

Fenton had met a great many such cases in real life; indeed, they formed the bulk of his murder investigations. He had opened locked rooms containing corpses which had been done to death by strangulation, shooting, stabbing, poison, smothering, drowning, burning, being chopped to bits, electrocution; by the action of deadly snakes and spiders – and far worse.

A few of such cases involved rooms which were not really locked at all. These included rooms with secret panels and one room where the midget assassin lay hidden in a chest. Fenton had left all such 'cheating' cases to the police.

More interesting were the cases where the rooms were really locked, but ingeniously locked from the outside. One killer, having simply locked the door and concealed the key in his hand, helped smash a panel of the door to get into the room. Then he reached through the panel and 'found' the key in the lock. Others relied on clever systems of string, pins, wires and so on, to drop latch-bars, shoot bolts and turn locks from outside the door. One killer simply removed the door hinges, replacing them after his grim business inside.

In other cases the room was locked, and from the inside, but it was not utterly unimpregnable. Poison gas might be introduced by a ventilator, as, indeed, might an adder. Ice bullets might be fired through the keyhole to kill, then melt, leaving no trace of the weapon. Others used poison darts fired through an otherwise inaccessible window, bombs down the chimney and so on. In one curious case a man was stabbed through the wall itself, with a very long, thin, sharp sword.

There were a number of 'funny contrivance' cases. These invariably concerned machines, hidden about the rooms which, having done their deeds, became to all appearances innocent furniture again. Some were set off by the victims themselves, some by remote control and some by clockwork. Men were shot by telephones, blown up by hearing aids, stabbed by clocks, strangled by stethoscopes and ripped to pieces by typewriters.

In this category Fenton placed his interesting 'Case of the Freudian Outlook', where a man was crushed to death between the red-hot iron walls of a gimmicked room.

He paused to cut a few more pages. This mystery, *The Locked Room*, was the most baffling he'd yet encountered, and nothing like any of the others.

It was certainly not like the elaborate suicide in 'The Mystery of the Yellow Step', where the victim hanged himself with an especially knotted and weighted rope. When the door to the room was broken in, this noose undid itself, deposited the body on the floor, and vanished out the window into (for this was in Venice) the Grand Canal.

Nor did this case resemble 'The Orchid Piano Mystery', where the victim locked himself in a room coincidentally full of broken furniture and other signs of a struggle, fainted and cracked his head on the fender. That case had given Fenton some food for thought, as had the related 'Mauve Marimba Mystery'. There the supposed victim had merely suffered an epileptic seizure, smashed up the room, and ended by kicking himself in the face until dead (this epileptic was also a dancer).

Fenton's meditations were here interrupted by Bozo, who came in with a tray of toast and cocoa.

'I was just thinking over some of my old "locked-room" cases, Bozo,' said the renowned gumshoe. 'I must confess that real-life cases are a whale of a lot easier than detective fiction. This novel has me stymied, so far.' And he outlined the story for his valet.

'It sounds tough, sir,' said Bozo. 'Reminds one of the "Case of the Bashful Bimbo".'

'No, I think you're thinking of the "Vast Duck Mystery", aren't you, Bozo? Where it finally turned out that the victim had been stabbed with a hatpin at the ambassador's reception, amid a roomful of people. He wasn't even aware of the stabbing himself. He'd gone into another room, locked himself in, and then the slow leakage from his heart finally caught up with him.'

'Like I've caught up with you,' laughed Inspector Grogan,

strolling in. 'I came over on the chance of getting you to help on the Stilton diamonds case. I found this young lady outside. Claims her life's in danger.'

The young lady, a beautiful blonde with a black eye, seemed too frightened to speak. Next came Claude Elliott, the millionaire playboy, attired in his customary black evening wear, a monocle twinkling in his eye. 'I say, old sport,' he drawled, 'd'you think you could do anything about it? Someone seems to have kidnapped Pater. His entire private car has vanished from its train. Deucedly awkward, what?' Young Elliott expected no answer to this question.

'Scuse me, mistah Wort',' said a jockey, ducking into view from behind Elliott's scarlet-lined cape. 'Honeymarch has been heisted!'

'Honeymarch stolen!' echoed the astonished shamus. This famous filly had won many times her weight in gold, as had her sire, My White Dream, which Fenton had earlier saved from doping in—

'The Case of the Mona Lisa Moth,' breathed Bozo.

'Exactly,' Fenton said. 'Get rid of some of these people – all of them, Bozo. I want to do some hard thinking.'

Bozo gently but firmly pushed them all from the library: the debutante and the B-girl, the Brovnian ambassador and the gum-chewing taxi driver, the business tycoon and the spirit medium, the jockey, the playboy, the cop and the black-eyed blonde.

'In "The Case of the Oddest Occurrence",' Fenton mused, 'the trick was to make it seem as if the victim were dead before he really was. The killer got him into a room and drugged him, and managed to get the room locked. Then he feigned alarm, convinced us there was something afoot, and broke the door down to get in. He rushed in ahead of us, I recall, exclaiming at the (fictitious) sight of the victim's throat, cut from ear to ear. And even while he was exclaiming, he was cutting that throat – an instant before the rest of us saw it!'

'It was another kettle of fish sir,' said Bozo, 'in the case you called "Murder Galore".'

'True enough, Bozo. In that, as in many cases, the ruse was to get the rest of us believing the victim to be still alive, when he had already been done to death. In the case you mention, this was accomplished by means of a phonographic recording of the victim's voice. Other cases involved the use of mirrors, disguises, death-masks and even ventriloquism. Yet *The Locked Room* is not one of this type.

'Nor does it resemble the more bizarre cases, such as "The Wrong Hotel Room Mystery", or the simpler ones, such as "The Case of the Gunsel's Gardenia". In the former the whole plot hinged upon an elaborate switch of door number plates; in the latter, the killer only *pretended* the door was locked, and held it shut as he feigned battering it open.'

Bozo withdrew, and the celebrated crime-solver locked and bolted the door. There remained only the pages of the final chapter to be cut, but he could not yet bring himself to break their seal. Surely he could guess the ending in advance of reading it! Surely, in all his experience, there must be one case relevant to solving this tangle.

Yet he had covered all categories: the secret passage or panel; the string-locked door; the ice bullet; and so on. There remained for consideration only one case, the strange 'Case of the Parched Adjutant'.

The Case of the Parched Adjutant

Another Fenton Worth Mystery

The victim was a retired military gentleman of sober and regular habits, an ardent anti-vivisectionist. He spent several hours each day in his study, writing his memoirs and anti-vivisection pamphlets, or perhaps just gazing out over the vast heath of which his window commanded an excellent prospect. When he was not writing, he could generally be found upon that heath, strolling and meditating. He had no relatives living, very little money, and a devoted housekeeper who was a chimpanzee.

On the day in question a circus had pitched on the heath, and the adjutant had, according to the housekeeper, gone to see it – for the second time. Worried at his absence, she finally called the police and Fenton Worth. No one at the circus had seen him. In search of the house, they broke in the door of his study.

The study had only one door, to which the adjutant had the only key, and its only window was inaccessible. The furniture consisted of a desk, a chair and a sofa. The adjutant was found lying on the sofa, strangled to death – with finger marks clear on his throat – and oddly parched. The door key was in his pocket.

The study window was open, but Fenton soon proved that it was inaccessible, for it lay forty feet above a mire of wet sand. This mire would neither support a ladder nor any climbing device, and its unbroken surface indicated that nothing had come within a hundred feet of the house on that side. It was further impossible to lower oneself from the roof by a rope, for the roof was made of treacherous rotten thatching – which likewise had not been disturbed.

A great deal of suspicion fell upon the housekeeper, as the adjutant's only heir. But an examination of the corpse, together with evidence from the adjutant's pamphlets and memoirs, established the true circumstances, as Fenton explained:

The adjutant had been strangled at the circus, bundled into a cannon, and fired through the window to land upon the sofa. This was confirmed by the parching, and powder burns on the corpse's feet. Certain details in the adjutant's memoirs and pamphlets showed that he had uncovered a vicious vivisection racket running behind the scenes at the circus, and was about to subject this sordid business to the light of public scrutiny. On his first visit to the circus, he had recognized an old enemy, an ex-Nazi artillery officer notorious during the war for his torture of animals, chiefly puppies and kittens. The adjutant's discovery of what the lions were fed completed his inquiry; the rest was duck soup, as he'd have said.

Confronted with this evidence, the Human Cannonball broke down and confessed, sobbing in half-coherent German.

'Hmmm,' said Fenton. 'Even that case doesn't help me here. Maybe I should re-read the novel, to see what clues I've missed.' The well-known peeper leafed back through the book.

'Say, here's an anomaly!' he exclaimed. 'The author tells us on page one the door is locked, and here on page three it so manifestly isn't! What can be the explanation of that?'

Suddenly the world-famed private eye sat bolt upright. 'Aha! The author says the door is locked, *but we have only his word for it.* The pieces of the jigsaw are beginning to fall into place, now. The author may in fact have *staged* the entire murder to make money from his own fictionalization of it! So the name of the killer must be—'

But the publicly-acclaimed private investigator will never name me. He'll be found tomorrow morning, stabbed to death, in a room locked from the inside. The *kriis* will have vanished.

Thus begins my novel of detection, another Fenton Worth Mystery.

Another Look

He took another look. This time he could see, on a shelf just inside the cabinet door, a tiny Zodiac arrangement: A circle divided into twelve sectors, each marked with symbols. He named them: bas, go, fen, dup, dor, pag, ut, lar, cav, mun-bas, bas-bas and go-bas. Odd, their having a naming system that used repetitions. The almanac didn't explain. They must have begun by naming something with fewer members – their eyes? – and then lazily, they'd transferred this system to everything. What the almanac was clear about was how it worked: The planet was supposed to make one half-turn each time this small brass arrow made one complete turn. No sense again. And the longer arrow ran through the Zodiac for every sector-movement of the small arrow – what a system! How did they ever manage to keep the planet revolving smoothly, as if running on the same think brass gears . . . not to mention a complete new moon, to be constructed every lar-go Zodiacs. No need to look further for an explanation of why they were extinct. Probably just ran out of money, as did so many human races. He noticed the arrows moving on into the sector 'cocktail hour'. That meant resetting his own Zodiac and

He took another look. In the middle distance stood a man looking at something reflected in a mirror. A dotted line ran from his triangular eye to the mirror and bounced to the far corner, where a breathing woman stood feeding the second dog. The first dog was gigantic. Perspective lines connected her nose, ear, collar with those of a tiny personoid near the horizon line. The man with the mirror was forming symbols overhead, words, he was counting backwards. He counted the breaths of the woman: dup, fen, go, bas . . . and at mun, she sank into the nearer part of the landscape. The dotted line swept and swept over the trees, hills, rayed sun, the half-eaten dog, but it failed to find her new location. Folding his mirror, the man shrank, flying back to the other far corner, where a cat waited to be fed.

He took another look. The experiment required him to stand perfectly still while a No. 13 bus rumbled downhill towards him. He drove the bus down the worn ruts, straight at the rigid figure (now it was not surprising that, as he moved forward in time, he moved forward, and the figure grew larger), while behind him passengers began to complain. 'I could have walked faster than this,' he said, peering over the driver's shoulder. 'Look at that crazy bastard looking at us.' 'I know what you mean,' he replied. The passenger ahead of him had picked his parachute to pieces – nerves, it hit a lot of them that way – and any moment, someone would mention the meals. 'And the meals they serve,' he said. 'I wouldn't feed those to an animal.' 'Who wouldn't feed an animal?' He couldn't hear what those ahead of him were talking about, but he could see them nodding. 'What was that? Did we hit something?' 'A dog?' They were all talking at once. 'Is this my stop? ' he asked, peering out the rear window. The whorls were unfamiliar, but the fort must be around here somewhere. He climbed down and watched the bus dust its way on down the hill, towards him. As it came closer he could see the grim driver, the excited passengers . . . he recalled the old trick: Look at the tyre treads, fix on them, look well into the herringbone pattern. As each pair of rubber rectangles hit the road, they squeeze up a tiny pinch of dirt between them. As the wheel turns on, they're released, they spring apart and puff the dirt into the air. 'What's he standing there looking at?'

He took another look. The encyclopedia (yes, another book – dusty books were all that remained of their strange race. There were times when he might have preferred a collection of stuffed reptiles, or an album of rare envelopes. It pleased him to think that they who made these books were now a part of the dust upon their pages) had prepared him for his encounter in the park. The girl would be waiting for him at A, the ice-cream vendor at B, the murderer with the bicycle at C. If he visited the girl or the ice-cream vendor first, the murderer would, as the encyclopedia put it, 'eliminate the other option'. But he could visit the murderer first, steal his bicycle, and pedal to loci A and B both, before the murderer could reach either locus on foot. As usual in such decisions, the greatest risk is attached to the greatest benefit. The problem seemed to involve every aspect of their primitive science: 'entropy' (the ice-cream was melting, the girl dying); criminology (the murderer very likely had a knife or a garrotte); geometry (the three points formed a triangle on a surface of unknown shape); even gyroscopic principles (he did not know how to ride a bicycle). On the shelf below the encyclopedia was a small mound of clay; looking closer, he saw that a tiny lay figure had climbed up on it and was about to speak. The lay figure opened his mouth and taught, saying: 'The kingdom of the next shelf is not like the kingdom of this shelf. The kingdom of the next shelf is like a ball-point pen that traces its own shadow. And when all the shadow is traced, the point is retracted, and the pen is clipped into a shirt pocket and forgotten. But the tracing is not forgotten.'

He looked again, taking a closer look at the book of fables, open on the polished oak table for anyone to see. Fables! Wasn't that like the human race, to waste their time on fables, when death rose like flying dust all about them. He knew now his own function, a useless robot, destined to keep opening the cabinet of himself and taking another look. But what use were fables, when silence, all through the fort, told him that this planet held no life. How did they all die? He wasn't sure about death, it wasn't as clear as life. Some may have died skewered by the black lines of bullets across the page, or some torn and tumbled by the jagged edges of explosions, red and orange with radial lines around the large red BLAM! Could any number of fat books of fables now bring them back for his inspection? He doubted it, even as he stepped forward to inspect the Table of Contents. It was almost completely blank by now, with the two remaining fables huddled at the bottom of the page, barely breathing. Turning quickly to the bayonet bookmark, he read THE EMU, THE AUK AND THE PASSENGER PIGEON: 'One day the emu, the auk and the passenger pigeon were arguing about the meaning of life. The passenger pigeon was easily the most clever, and the other two were finally struck speechless by the brilliance of his argument. Then, just as he spread his wings to make a final dramatic point, the pigeon slipped, fell over, struck his head on the fender, and died. "Pity," said the Great Auk. "Last of his kind, wasn't he?" "I think he had a wife somewhere," replied the emu. "But they haven't been living together for years. Still, we'll never see his like again. What an argument!" The Great Auk preened. "Oh, I don't know. There's such a thing as being too smart for your own good."' The next story, THE FOX AND THE ERASER, was fading fast. 'One day a fox, finding a vain and idle eraser, decided to play a trick on the slow-witted object. "Can you erase *anything*?" he asked. "Of course I can." "Then how about erasing this fable?" "Nothing easier. If I can't erase this fable, I'll give you anything you like – my daughter's hand in marriage." "Agreed," said the wily ox, and the era immediately busied himself with the able. In nc tim at al, th e hd cmpltly obltrtd evrythng but—' The blank page was thinner, and the whole book seemed to be wearing away to dust. Erasers have a terrible way, he recalled, of working at pictures as well as words. The shine vanished from the oak, and the oak from the fort, and the fort from the terrible silence, as he took another look.

Space Shoes of the Gods
An Archaeological Revelation

Why do so many ancient legends speak of gods who fly in flaming chariots? Why is the Great Pyramid built strong enough to withstand an H-bomb blast? What possible connection can there be between Easter Island, Stonehenge, and the messages received on my Aunt Edna's ouija board? Orthodox scientists are unable, perhaps unwilling, to answer such daring questions.

Of course it's never easy to abandon our old misconceptions and accept fresh ideas. Scientists bitterly attacked Galileo when he proved that the Leaning Tower of Pisa was a pendulum. They pooh-poohed Darwin's revolutionary notion that mankind is descended from the beagle. They laughed themselves sick at Edison's light bulb, as they will at any brilliant idea eons ahead of its time.

My idea, for instance. I do not expect understanding from the narrow-minded men of the scientific establishment. They are too busy pottering around with test tubes in musty laboratories to listen to anything new and important. Rather, my article is directed to those young, adventurous minds who are not afraid to believe the impossible. I am in the position of the first beagle who dared to walk on his hind legs, so to speak. No doubt there was some smart beagle professor standing by, to call him a crank and a dreamer. All the same, he took that first great step.

Today we are taking another great step, a giant step from Earth[1] into the vast spaces of space. Yet how much do we really know about this universe of ours, with its dozens on dozens of galaxies, each packed with scores of literal stars?

Earthbound science has no answers. But a few far-sighted 'cranks and dreamers' have ventured to say that:

a. There are certainly other civilizations in the universe *exactly like ours*, if not more so.

b. *They* are trying desperately to get in touch with us, perhaps to borrow money.

c. *They* must have landed here on Earth in the prehistoric past.

d. Wherever *They* landed, *They* were worshipped as gods by the natives. Their modern equipment, which would seem prosaic to us, must have been fearful magic for our ancestors. Imagine, for example, how the simple Egyptians might have reacted to gods carrying ballpoints, credit cards and contact lenses!

e. For some reason, the space gods wearied of all this worship, and departed.

Hard to believe? Orthodox science may try to dismiss such notions with a wave of its oscilloscope. But then orthodox science still cannot explain away certain facts . . .

The Evidence

Last year, English miners opened a seam of coal 15 million years old. Inside, they found the clear fossil imprint of *a modern zipper.*

How could it have got there? Did an ancient space visitor with zipper pockets on his uniform fall asleep in the English jungle, never to awaken? Was he left behind by the expedition? Could he have been murdered by one of his space brothers?[2]

Conventional scientists have their own 'explanation' of this strange anthracite evidence. They call it a fossil fern. But they have yet to explain what a fern was doing wearing a uniform with zipper pockets.

In the same way, conventional archaeologists have tried to explain away a remarkable cave drawing found in Blague, France. They call it 'a hunter shooting game with a bow and arrow'. But the hunter's bow looks astonishingly like a modern sextant, to the unprejudiced eye of this non-scientist. The drawing can only be a space navigator taking bearings on a woolly mammoth. Museums are filled with similar archaeological mistakes; Stone 'spearheads' which, as anyone can see, are actually stone letter-openers.

The ancient world abounds in such unexplained mysteries. How could the simple inhabitants of Easter Island have carved their enormous stone faces and heaved them into place, without the aid of rock drills and bulldozers? How could gigantic pyramids have been built by the primitive, cave-dwelling Egyptians? Science has not begun to unravel the mystery of the pyramids, nor even to solve the riddle of the Sphinx.

A ruined edifice in Peru bears a weird inscription: two horizontal lines crossed by two vertical lines. In other words, the figure for tic-tac-toe, *a game played by the latest giant computers.* Likewise the Ankara Museum displays clay tablets pierced with holes – the same holes used in modern IBM cards. Could this represent the payroll arrangements of our cosmic visitors?

Peculiar Roundnesses

The jungles of Costa Rica are littered with mysterious stone balls, some of them larger than Volkswagens. I spoke with the amateur archaeologist who is studying these curious rock spheres in connection with his search for Martin Bormann.

'I can't really understand these odd orbs,' he confided. 'According to a local legend, these uncanny globes fell from the sky. The native name for them translates as "strange spheroids". Could they be small planets from some lesser solar system? At this stage, we can't rule out anything, even the possibility that some vanished race of giants played marbles here.'

Two intriguing ideas. Controversy rages on between the odd-ball planet theory and the lost-marble theory, but one question must be answered:

If these are tiny planets, what has become of their even tinier inhabitants?

The roundness theme appears again in the art of many cultures. Australian aborigines, among others, have drawn circles on pieces of wood. A ceremonial frieze of ancient Mexico, which is covered with circles, undoubtedly depicts traffic lights, ball bearings, embroidery, hoops, curly hair and many other items not re-discovered until the twentieth century.

My list could go on to include hundreds of these anachronisms, but I will end it with an object in my own collection. Not long ago I acquired a small Indo-Sumerian statue of bronze. Purblind anthropologists would probably call it a 'fertility goddess', ignoring certain features which are obvious to any child:

On the chest of the goddess are two distinct, modern doorbells.

The Legends

In the light of evidence like the above, we might re-examine some of the legends of the so-called past. Take the Nordic sagas for example. There we read of strange gods who drank from horns. Virgil, too, speaks of dreams coming through a gate of horn, while the Book of Revelation describes gates of pearl. From Shakespeare we hear the legend of the base Indian who threw away a pearl, while many Indian myths speak of peculiar gods. Can all this be coincidence? No, it is far more likely that these myths convey primitive ideas of television, twin-tub washing machines and electric toothbrushes.[3] This is confirmed in Genesis, where we read of an angel (a technician) who guarded the gates of Eden (spaceship) with a flaming sword (soldering iron).

Finally we are confronted with the 'wild' tales of the early Spanish conquistadores, who swore they found in America men with feathers growing right out of their heads! Who were these odd feather-headed strangers, and what were they doing on our planet?

The Lost Galaxy

By now it must be plain that many of our space gods were tourists. In the distant past, Earth was no doubt a tourists' paradise, an unspoiled wilderness where the featherheads could get away from their own crowded galaxy. They may have built themselves a few amenities, such as the pyramid saunas of Egypt, or Stonehenge (a luxury motel), but they left most of the planet delightfully wild.

What spoiled it for them? The Deluge? The sinking of the luxury liner *Atlantis*? Whatever the reason, our cosmic tourists departed, leaving behind only a few traces: a zipper jacket in England, marbles in Costa Rica, a crumpled kleenex (now to be seen at the Stockholm Museum of Antiquities, in a wastebasket near the door).

Some uncanny tourist instinct must have told them that Earth was doomed.[4] The natives were getting too civilized. All too soon earthlings would cover the paradise planet with highways and fuming traffic; fill its air with thundering jets carrying earthling tourists; and pack its universities with so-called professors who scoff at my theory.

The space gods have left our solar system and gone back to work. But someday – when we have finally rid this planet of evil, pollution, war, disease and skeptical scientists – then our gods will return.[5] They will bring us all the benefits of their superior civilization. They will shower us with plenty of valuable cargo.

Notes

1. The question of giants *in* the Earth will be taken up in a later monograph.
2. Just such a space-brother murder could well account for the strange legend of Cain and Abel. I have communicated my suspicions to Scotland Yard, urging them to examine the coal deposits for fossil fingerprints. So far, they have remained ominously silent on the matter.

3. Further confirmation is provided by the certain knowledge that Shakespeare's base Indian threw his pearl *before swine.* This proves that Shakespeare's plays were really written by Bacon, a space visitor.

4. 'Tourist instinct' is an example of clairvoyance, or 'knowing' that something will go wrong just before it does. I refer the reader to an interesting experiment at Earl University, where a researcher asks subjects to drop buttered toast and predict whether it will land face-down or face-up. So far, the experiment is a failure, Dr Bormann reports. But he adds, 'The interesting thing is, *I just knew it would fail.*'

5. Some doddering scientists sneer at the idea of travel between stars. The nearest star, they say, is 25 trillion miles away. They forget that monorail trains are capable of astonishing speeds (over 200 m.p.h.!). Doubtless, despite the skeptics, we'll have a regular train service to Alpha Centauri and other stars, by the end of the century.

The Poets of Millgrove, Iowa

Throw Away That Truss

The Astronaut was almost happy about having decapitated a mole while shaving. He'd always wanted to use one of those peculiarly-shaped patches that come in the Bandaid assortment. But when he dug down in the flight bag and came up with the tin box, he found it empty.

'Jeanne,' he muttered.

'What?' Jeanne spread a drop of enamel on her toenail and thrust out her foot to inspect it.

'Did we carry an empty tin Bandaid box all the way from California?' Without waiting for the obvious answer, he went into the bathroom, stuck a piece of toilet paper over the wound, and began brushing his teeth electrically. The noise cut off the radio's words from the bedroom, and he found himself alone with his face.

The Astronaut's face, if shaved by a Gillette blade, could have aroused bubbles of admiration from the head of an oil millionaire's daughter: 'Hmmm, not bad-looking, either!' (But not, he thought, with a piece of bloody toilet paper glued to it.) It featured a square, pink jaw terminating in a chin like a ripe apricot, superbly cloven. His nostrils were slightly flared, sensing danger, his eyebrows seriously straight and incapable of mockery, and his forehead – whatever a forehead should be – intelligent, he guessed. Even his teeth were proper reminders of death, orderly rows of military tombstones.

Today, however, his face showed classic lines of 'nervous tension'. He and Jeanne had travelled two thousand miles to his home town, where he was born but not raised, so that he could give his speech at the Millgrove Harvest Festival. So that Jeanne could paint her nails and worry about losing her tan. His own tan was turning yellow, he noted, unplugging the razor.

'—a modern miracle!' the radio blurted.

The Astronaut rolled deodorant under each arm and behind his knees.

For Teenagers With Troubled Skin

He had left her alone in the MILLGROVE MOTE, as the faulty neon sign told her, and Jeanne, examining her toes, remembered she had nothing to read. There was only the worn and stained copy of *Popular Mechanics* by the toilet. Seated, wearing her patented lastex with fiberfil inserts, kolitron panels, nickel-chrome and neoprene clips, six-way stretch girdle that b-r-e-a-t-h-e-d, Jeanne read how to build her own. She yawned over elaborate schematic diagrams and finally turned to: 'Honey, I got the job!' – a man embraced a woman who smiled and raised one foot from the floor. The woman, smiling, embraced the smiling man with his hand, embracing her, clutching a rolled-up newspaper. Smiling, they embraced. He embraced this woman with her foot raised in salute.

Jeanne saw the man had chosen one of the following occupations:

Accounting
Advanced Mathematics
Advertising
Air Conditioning

Tool Design
Welding Processes
Yard Maintenance
Zoo Sanitary Engineering

But after all, as the magazine indicated, life is what you convert it into, what you Bild-UR-Self. The radio played the opening chords of a song about a hot rod, and Jeanne's girdle s-i-g-h-e-d.

Nothing to Buy

'It don't make you – you know – sterile, does it?' asked the grinning sheriff.

The Astronaut shook his head, then turned its profile to the older man and bent over his coke.

'That's all right then.'

In the rear of the store the druggist, Bud Goslin, his glasses glittering, moved among his glittering bottles of vitamins. He hummed a tune the Astronaut could not identify.

The Kind of Girl Tab Hunter Wants

Jeanne picked at the polish on her toenail. At home, the water in the pool would be turning brown and filthy, like the ook in the bottom of the golf bag in the garage. Nola has the key, she thought. Nothing can possibly happen. I'm getting a cold.

The radio gave a recipe. Jeanne wondered how Fritz, her dog, was getting along.

She saw what she had done and took out the bottle of polish remover.

Sodium Propionate Added, to Retard Spoilage

The Astronaut's gesture took in rubber syringes, steel nail files, lavender soap, paragoric, kleenex, comic books, morphine, green stamps, and the hidden drawer of condoms.

'There is a certain poetry in all this,' he said. The grinning sheriff nodded, and he went on, 'a certain poetry. Yes, a certain poetry. You know?' The grinning sheriff and Bud Goslin both nodded.

Teen Queen Screen Dream was the magazine the young girl held. Dropping a quarter in Bud Goslin's hand, she glided toward the door.

'All the nice young nooky come in here,' said the sheriff, grinning at his lemon phosphate.

'I know, I know.'

Bud Goslin came from behind his counter and rushed at the kids sitting in the floor.

'If you kids don't want to buy any,' he said, 'you can't sit here reading them all day.' He snatched the comics from them and herded the boys out the door. The air-conditioning made a faint coughing sound.

'Christ, I wish I was thirty years younger. All the nice young nooky come in here,' said the grinning sheriff.

What am I doing here? the Astronaut asked himself. This is not my town. I was not raised here, only born here.

But he felt the same about the town in which he was raised. This is not my town, what am I doing here? he thought, in London and New York and Menominee, Wisconsin.

In front of the courthouse stood a raw wood platform, from which the Astronaut would 'launch' his speech, as the mayor put it. Jeanne would not be there, for reasons of her own. They would give him the key to the city, and the poets of Millgrove would read poems in his honour. He would give his speech, and then they would hang him, as in *Untamed Town*, the innocent man they hang, and all day he listens to them building the raw wood scaffold . . .

He stood up and reached in his pocket.

'Your money's no good,' said the druggist.

Count the Number of Beans in this Jar

I'll kill him, thought Jeanne, painting her toenails Kotton Kandy. The right foot smeared on the bed. Going on and leaving me without anything to read.

When the polish had dried, she slipped on her sandals and the peasant skirt and the acetate blouse, and went next door to the Sof-Top Ice Cream stand. The rays of the setting sun made her white blouse glow pink. She drank a cup of coffee at the picnic table and watched the sunset. Mosquitoes clung to the warmth of her arms. The girl behind the counter read *The New Liz*, wetting her thumb to turn the pages. A motorcycle went by, and the rider waved to the girl behind the counter. She did not look up. It was dark enough for Jeanne to remove the sunglasses she'd bought in Paris, but she left them in place. Fritz is at Nola's, she assured herself. Nothing can possibly happen.

Astonishing and Unbelievable!

The parade came by the bunting-draped platform slowly at first; a file of doll-buggies draped in bunting. Little girls dressed in white pushed bunting-draped buggies containing plastic dolls past the platform of wood, draped in bunting. Some of the little girls cried, and their mothers removed them from the parade. Others glided smoothly past, walking to an invisible rhythm, pushing buggies past the mayor, the grinning sheriff, the grinning wife of the mayor, the sheriff's wife, Bud Goslin, and the Astronaut.

The Astronaut wore a dress uniform and saluted when the flag went by. The Millgrove High School band went by, playing 'Them Bases'. The Astronaut, seeing his country's flag, saluted it, and the flag was carried by, along with the flag of Millgrove High School, green and red. A woman across the street wore Jeanne's french sunglasses, the Astronaut saw.

A series of antique cars passed, each one exactly like the one before. Then came a float depicting the Harvest Festival: corn and pumpkins spilling out of a cornucopia held by Betty Mason, queen of the Harvest Festival. The American Legion followed, marching to some invisible, inaudible rhythm of their own, and the Astronaut saluted his country's flag.

The crowd gathered around the bunting-draped platform, while the mayor raised and lowered the adjustable microphone several times.

'Testing,' he breathed cautiously into it, and an unearthly howl went up from the loudspeakers. Bud Goslin dropped to one knee beside the amplifier box. Light blazed from his glasses. He stood up.

'Testing,' said the mayor once more, and his amplified voice shouted from the speakers. Chuckling, he added, 'Five, four, three, two, one.' The crowd laughed.

'Well, I hope everyone is having a good time, here,' said the mayor. 'I know I am.'

A hundred pairs of silver sunglasses tilted to look at him.

'Yes, we're here to celebrate our tenth annual Harvest Festival, and if you ain't having a good time, I say it's your own darned fault!' The crowd smiled.

'We have with us a young man I'm sure all of you know. A boy who was born right here in Millgrove, a real down-to-earth fella—' He paused, while the crowd laughed very hard.

'—seriously though, a boy who represents all that is fine about our town, a boy who has done more, seen more, and I guess travelled more than any of us ever will: Our Astronaut!'

The crowd clapped.

'Bud Goslin here – Bud Goslin—' said the mayor over their noise, '—Bud has written a little poem in Our Astronaut's honour. Bud?'

The druggist stood up, looking ashamed, and read rapidly from a paper:

Our Astronaut

He soars far upward in the night,
He comes back safe, to our greatest delight.
He's the finest boy that Millgrove has got,
So let's give a big cheer for our Astronaut!

Bud sat down amid mild applause.

'And now, Mr Fenner, Hal Fenner of the High School English Department, has another poem for our boy,' said the mayor. Mr Fenner was quite young, but had a moustache. His poem was untitled.

'Hail to thee, blithe astronaut,' it began. After a number of puzzling references to the Confederate dead, it finished, '. . . blazing a heavenly trail!'

'And now a word from our guest of honour,' the mayor announced. The Astronaut walked militarily to the microphone and waited until the applause died.

'I don't know what you came out here to hear,' he said. 'Let me start like this:

'All this pigs**t you hear about astronauts is so much f**king – uh – s**t. What the f**k, a guy goes up inside this little metal room, see, it don't mean a f**k of a lot. Any f**king body could do it, you see what I mean?'

'Look out, mister,' said a hoarse voice at his feet. 'There's a lot of *women* here.'

'They put you through a lot of f**king tests and all, but what the f**k. Any f**king asshole with two eyes and two hands could operate the c**ksucker. F**king A. All you got is this f**king little—'

'You tell 'em, captain,' said a young man in a motorcycle jacket. He had his arm around the woman in the french sunglasses. The grinning sheriff was no longer grinning.

'—this f**king little board with some motherf**king little red and green lights on it, see? And you just throw switches to keep the green lights on. Christ-all-f**king-mighty, even this c**ksucking fairy teacher, with his blithe f**king spirit, could operate the f**ker.'

The sheriff stood up, as a man in mirror sunglasses yelled, 'We don't talk that way in front of ladies, Mister.' The entire crowd was murmuring, not listening now, but only trying to see what was going to happen to him.

'He's drunk!' a woman screamed.

The sheriff got a hammer lock on the Astronaut and eased him away from the microphone. The mayor came forward and adjusted it several times, saying, 'Well, folks, I guess our boy was still flying too high, heheh.' He was preparing to entertain them with a few imitations, when he discovered he still held the large, wooden, gold-painted key. He walked back to drop it disgustedly on the empty seat, and stood for a moment, watching the Astronaut and the sheriff descend from the platform. The mayor returned to the microphone, saying, 'Speaking of high flyers, have you ever heard a chicken hawk? I guess most of you have, and he sounds something like this:'

Then the mayor screamed.

The Commentaries

1. The Lost Wind, *by Stefan Berg*
Reviewed by Lionel Eps

Berg loved word-play. As his diary shows, he fiddled with intricate word-games through his last days at San Esteban prison. The diary itself remains to be published; perhaps when it is, some light will be shed upon the 'conspiracy' theory so beloved of Mr Grice.

THE LOST WIND plays not only with words, but with itself. Joycean paronomasia is one thing, but what are we to make of lines like these:

> shine handy donor fucks, halters, coarsely talls
>
> A Mr Oops laminates set animal spoor, Ma.
>
> No authory tease are so convincting as the
> evidunce of I's i's.

The decipherment effort is often not worth the result, the games not worth the tangle.

We are in no better luck in understanding the story. Presumably it is someone's journal (whose?) though we never learn whose (mine?). The narrator is imprisoned, or waiting to be born, or locked in a mental ward, or one of the other tiresome excuses for a long, boring 'experiment', and he is of course a novelist. This is supposed to be his diary (and how much more to the point it would have been to have given us Berg's actual diary!), and it contains several scrappy novel plots and even plots within plots.

One loses the whole thread amid surreal nonsense, anecdotes

about some pre-posthumous tribe called the Iructu, fake 'reviews' of unwritten works, and of course a dream. Nowhere is it explained what the title zephyr is, if anything. The whole is so filled with empty puns, misprints and weak jokes that finally one is tempted to call the lost wind a sparrow fart an afflatus to retitle it a Breaking Wind not to care if it is a hurricaine or a sparrow fart.

2. The Lost Wind, *by Steven Burg*
Reviewed – by H. Truice

It is surprising that so eminent a critic as Mr Eps cannot understand this novel, and that he pretends to be perplexed even by simple palindromes and lines such as

thine sandy honor ducks, falters, hoarsely calls

THE LOST WIND is a chinese box of a novel, a tidy though intricate palimpsest, a cry of hope and despair, mouthed by a man condemned, as are we all. The wind that blows through this thinking reed can make it sing. Far from a bit of literary self-abuse, this is a darksome mirror, a foil-etched overview of mankind-here symbolized by the Iructu tribe. As we all know, the Iructu have no word for 'man', but use a native vegetable word in its place.

Appropriately enough, the novel ends in the prison cafeteria, where everyone is eating dessert.

3. The Lost Wind, *by S. Burke*
Reviewed by G. Grice

Through the lens of a handful of comic reviews, Burke reveals his well-wrought and deep-running novel, the story of an imprisoned writer known only as G.

G, condemned to death, plans a last novel, though there will be no time to write it. The story is that of a disturbed man, a writer named Garber. The significance of this name becomes apparent at once; Garber clothes his fantasies as a dream from which he awakens and begins to write. We are not told what the dream is until the end.

Garber's novel, *The Conspiracy*, concerns three writers who meet at a seaside convention: Eps, Griver and Barge. Griver is very old and very famous, yet somehow unsatisfied. He has long dreamt of creating an artificial historical event, a 'history within the interstices of History'. Eps is a middle-aged hack and amateur anthropologist who wishes to someday write a book about a fictitious tribe called the Iructu. Barge is a young poet with a correspondingly larger dream: the invention of an undiscovered land, complete with flora and fauna ('he could see bowers of red frimsia, fragrant parson's shoe, and the ancient ground-clinging bridesblood').

The three agree to collaborate on a mammoth scheme: Each will write his dream book, and each will allude directly and indirectly to those of the others. Together they will create a new world.

Griver expresses misgivings; at 96 he has not long to live, and there is some doubt he will complete his part of the project.

Here there is a compound hiatus in the manuscript(s). Garber's telephone rings and continues ringing as he tries to ignore it. G's guard comes to tell him his last appeal has failed. The story of Garber ducks, falters, hoarsely calls to him, and then is swept on. Here too there is a hiatus in the

as G's head is being shaved, he has Garber answer the phone. Long-distance from Porlock, Maine. The three in *The Conspiracy* appear to have succeeded, for the public is beginning to speculate about the reality of the Iructu, their land, their history. It is unclear how Garber wrote all this while the phone went on ringing – perhaps this is a different time – but he answers it:

'A person from Porlock!' Garber carved. 'Self!'

'I'm kidding, it's me, Hannah.' Otto Hannah was his publisher, a man fond of literary indicates. 'I want you to drop around to my office sometime next berg. I have something to discuss with you.'

'I'm going to an execution Mon. How about Tues?'

But when he arrived at the imposturing office, Hannah was out. A manuscript lay on the familiarly desk, and, with an afflatus of dread, Garber turned it around and began reading.

SOLITAIRE

a novel by H. Truice

And on page 4 was Garber's own dream, 'Jelly Days'.

Hannah comes in. He has forgotten, or pretends to forget, the purpose of the appointment. Reluctant to talk about the novel or its author, he tries to brush off Garber. They quarrel. Finally Garber leaves, having surreptitiously pocketed the first few pages of the manuscript. He flings out of the office at 11:59 a.m., July 2, 1961, gets into an elevator and goes into a daydream:

All over the city, businessmen begin rummaging through their files. What is it they are looking for? Their secretaries stand by, asking if they can help, but the bosses cannot describe the object.

G is taken to be executed. In his last few minutes, he thinks of Garber writing of the conspirators writing of the friendly Iructu:

Death is never referred to by name among the Iructu. Instead they use 'potato' imagery. Dying is called 'eating your potatoes', burial is 'planting the potatoes', a stillborn child is a 'new potato', and so on.

Garber reaches the ground floor, crosses the lobby, steps out into the sunshine and sees the bleeding corpse of Hannah. G recalls striking out a frivolous line about the publisher's having 'finally achieved an editorial miracle: going over forty stories in two minutes.'

Garber's defense counsel is a young cousin named Barker. He encourages him to plead guilty: a fatal mistake. Barker tries to make much of the symmetry of the situation – the murder of a man with two palindromic names exactly halfway through one of those rare years readable upside-down – all this is used as evidence of obsession.

G dies:

To break wind is considered a frightening event, and cause for mourning among one's relatives. The Iructu believe the soul may accidently leave the body through the anus, giving a ghastly cry as it goes. Chronic flatulence is looked on as a serious disease, and the Iructu understood only too well when I described to them the death of Athanasius, the theologian who exploded in his privy.

Reviewers begin to argue over the meaning of G's posthumously-published novel. Sections of it seem to be plagiarized from *Plague of Chance*, by Steve Bragg, in particular the final portion, the 'Jelly Days' dream.

Garber appeals, and a curious arrangement of circumstances defeats him. His lawyer loses several pages of the brief he is to lay before the judge. The judge is old and hard of hearing. The district attorney is suffering from piles and inclined to be vindictive. Scanning the partial brief, the judge believes he is presiding over a plagiarism case. He misses much of young Barker's eloquence and finds for the piles.

'A travesty of justice!' Barker called out, but the judge had already turned away and was descending. There was no one to hear but the DA, who, with a beatific smile, was sitting very straight and sliding back and forth in his chair. This motion is called among the Iructu 'duck-calling'; it is used in wind-easing ceremonies.

4. Plague of Chance, *by Steve Bragg*
Reviewed by H. Carver

Bragg makes use of trivial word-games ('So many dynamos!' 'She bears each cross patiently'), the device of a set of reviews and a set of novels to convey an unnecessary and false vision of rebirth. He pretends the frimsia is not a flower and the Iructu not a South American tribe, while ample references to these can be found in the works of Eps and Hannah. Dotted with improbable names, plotless and humorless, PLAGUE OF CHANCE is scarcely workable. The ending dream is nice, though by the time it arrives no one cares.

5. The Commentaries, *by H. Otto*
Reviewed by Hannah Berg

I have been asked to review this work – though I can hardly do so fairly – because of the controversy that has arisen regarding the dream sequence. I will not cry 'plagiarism' or attack Otto – poor mad condemned soul – but simply reproduce here the version of 'Jelly Days' which appeared in my own earlier novel. No authorities are so convincing as the evidence of one's eyes.

A mixture of *Castle of Otranto* and *Turn of the Screw*, at first. There are two secretive children and some mysterious (not always gigantic) manifestations: Someone in the house reaches into a cupboard to pick up something, and a giant hand reaches in the window and snatches someone away, or almost. The giant hand is that of the children's dead brother. Once a peculiar rocket-plane zooms in. It is painted in childish toy colours: red/white striped wings, yellow wheels, blue fuselage. Flapping its wings (in imitation of a visible gull) it skims low over the great interior fields.

Of the children's whispered conversations, the only words which can be distinguished are 'jelly days'. I leave the house to return to my childhood. Ed Hand is still running the Teeny Weeny Grocery store. Looking in the window, I see he is discussing some historical event with someone.

I am projected back to the event. A sign carries a book club advertisement I recently saw:

accept as a GIFT
Lucretia Borgia

An Italian political quarrel: One man is to be put to death in the restaurant kitchen, in this way: His body has been marked with horizontal lines into ten zones. He is to be shot in one zone, allowed to heal, then shot in the next zone (head, then neck, then chest . . .). The waiters deny this plot, and even the victim tries to cover it up.

I discover that I am dead. I do not know how I came to die,

or how I know I'm dead. Perhaps I am talking to someone and realize they are not listening.

Deathland is very pleasant and ordinary. Everyone has to work at their former job, more or less. Sociologists are very much in demand, the place seems like a kibbutz, very jolly and industrious, equipped with many wall charts.

It seems one can only communicate with the living through accidents and imitation. At last I understand what 'jelly day' means. It is of course just the day one leaves one's mortal jelly.

We gather in the cafeteria in the evening to watch a TV play about the end of the world. In the play, the actors tune in to Radio 4 to catch the end-of-the-world news.

On a hunch, I tune in to Radio 4 myself. But there is nothing unusual on, just the same bouncy Muzak tunes I expected.

Then I realize that this *is* the news – ordinary, palling life goes right on, up to the last moment. As I realize it, I hear thousands of footsteps coming downstairs into the cafeteria. The new crowds are arriving. It is everyone's jelly day.

6. . . .
Reviewed by . . .
. . . until finally:

until finally the endless criticism does end. The ship sets out to discover this land, these people, the traces of this event. It is left to the reader (Garber) to determine whether or not they succeed.

Heavens Below
Fifteen Utopias

Getting There Is $\left(\frac{n-1}{n}\right)$ *th the Fun*

Professor Lodeworm made one last adjustment. 'If my Utopia-ray works according to plan,' he said, 'it should make life for everyone a continual round of delightful anticipation, ever closer and closer to satisfaction. Now I'll switch it on.'

Professor Lodeworm made one last adjustment. 'If my Utopia-ray works according to plan,' he said, 'it should make life for everyone a continual round of delightful anticipation, ever closer and closer to satisfaction. Now I'll switch it on.'

The Bright Side

On Dr Freeman's desk at the Astronomy Institute we found a list headed 'UTOPIAS'. The first items were:

1. Arrange the planets in order of size, of color, of mass, and in alphabetical order.
2. The world population, laid end to end, ought to reach about eleven or twelve times to the moon. Test this.
3. Make friends with a black hole.
4. Adjust the earth's rotation so that my watch always keeps perfect time.
5. Land a man on the sun.
6. Carve Mercury, Venus, Earth, and Mars with the faces of Washington, Jefferson, Lincoln, and Theodore Roosevelt.
7. Paint the moon's bright side black.

The remainder of this list was obscured by blood from Dr Freeman's throat. He lay with his head on the desk, having apparently killed himself with a piece of broken glass. We think the glass came from the objective lens of the Institute telescope, which he'd smashed earlier in the day.

A talk with his physician cast more light on the matter. He had diagnosed in Dr Freeman a deterioration of the optic nerve.

'I can understand an astronomer's being unhappy at going blind,' he explained. 'Wish I hadn't told him to look on the . . .'

Mr and Ms America

'I know they always say it's hard to be a judge in these contests,' George said. 'But you know, it really is hard. Hell, we've got at least fifteen possibles here, and they all look good to me.'

Lotte yawned. 'Not to me. Vanity surgery isn't much, nowadays. Look, each of these characters has sunk half a million in his own body, and what have they really got? Look at this one, now.'

Mr Florida was parading above them. George saw little enough wrong with him. With Mr Florida's three-foot coxcomb, rib fins, and real eyes set into his female breasts, he was at least the Number Three contender.

Ms South Dakota looked even better. She had restricted herself to a hundred pounds of implanted fat, extra fingers and toes, and a small, shapely pair of antlers.

Next came Ms Iowa, an atavism of the 1950s: ninety-inch bust, ten-inch waist, thirty feet of trailing blonde hair, and feet equipped with tall spike heels. A decided washout, along with Mr Alaska and his fifty-pound penis that looked like a case of elephantiasis, nothing more.

By lunchtime, they'd narrowed it down to five men and four women. George and Lotte agreed the contest was tawdry, grotesque, and decadent. Over lunch, they tried to puzzle out what was wrong.

'The trouble is,' George said, 'most of the young surgeons have no ideas. Laszlo Goodwin's okay, but the rest – amateur copyists.'

'Not like our day,' Lotte said. 'Your outfit still looks good, you know?'

'Thanks. Yes, old Morton knew his stuff. A simple concept like this never looks out-of-date: seal fur all over, eyes on stalks, and a toroidal torso. My tailor says it's a real pleasure and a challenge, making clothes for a man with a big hole through his middle. But you still look great, too.'

'Thanks,' said Lotte. She cut a bite of steak and delicately stuffed it up her armpit.

Empty Promise

'Just sign here,' said the Devil, 'and name your wish.'

Jonathan Palmer sighed. 'I wish for Utopia,' he said. 'A perfect world without blemish or unpleasantness.'

'But—' said the Devil, looking surprised as he vanished forever.

'Things seem better already,' said Jonathan Palmer as he vanished forever.

'Better and better,' said his wife, turning from the keyhole to embrace her lover, Raoul. As she vanished forever, Raoul recalled that he was the sole beneficiary of her sizable insurance policy. He immediately vanished, followed by the cunning insurance salesman, his grasping boss, and the rest of imperfect humanity.

I alone am left. Ha-ha—

The Paradise Problem

Blenheim won his island by correctly guessing the number of coffee beans in a boxcar. He named his utopian republic Boxcar, its capital, Bean.

The island population consisted of two tribes, the Ye (who always told the truth) and the Ne (who always lied). A man from one tribe or the other was always posted at a fork in the main road, where one branch led to the city, the other into cannibal country.

By the river, Blenheim found a party of missionaries and cannibals, waiting to row across. The rowboat could carry only two men. If the cannibals on either shore outnumbered the missionaries, they would eat them.

Farther down the river was a pair of men with the curious names of A and B. A could evidently row upstream half as fast as B could swim downstream, while A and B together could row upstream twice as fast as B alone.

The two men explained that they were always engaging in contests, such as chopping wood, pumping water, racing a bicycle against a car, and so on. B was as many years older than A as A's age had been when B was as old as A was when B gave him half his apples plus half an apple.

In the city of Bean, the baker, draper, tailor, and smith were named (not respectively) Baker, Draper, Tailor, and Smith. Baker was the tailor's uncle, and Draper was the smith's son. Tailor had no living relatives. If Draper was the tailor, then the smith was named after the occupation of the man named after the occupation of Draper. Otherwise, the city was very beautiful.

Blenheim spent many happy years in Boxcar, drawing various colored socks out of a drawer in order to get a matching pair. Exactly how many happy years did he spend?

What Changed Doyster's Mind

Doyster stepped out of his time machine and strolled up the shady avenue of the Academy grove to Plato's house. The philosopher was just now supervising workmen who were placing a lintel over the door. On the lintel was inscribed: 'Let no one enter here who is unacquainted with geometry.'

'It won't work, boss,' called one of the men. 'The posts are too far apart. It won't reach across.'

'Nonsense,' said Plato. 'Let go your end.'

As one end of the lintel crashed to the ground, Doyster was already walking back down the shady avenue.

Handout

The League of Nations rules put it like this: Everyone in the world was entitled to go along to his nearest Dispensary and collect, free, a large box of God.

The first problem was a big riot in South America, owing to a rumor that supplies were running out. The League made a reassuring broadcast: No shortage was imminent. Indeed, the supply was expected to last indefinitely.

The riots in the Indian subcontinent were harder to combat. Local officials began to gripe: 'Oh, sure, there's enough to go around, but it's not in the right places. Rich Americans have enough to burn, while poor Indians are shelling out a hundred rupees a box on the black market. Is that justice? Why can't we straighten out the distribution?'

The League looked into it, and sent a memo: God was already present everywhere in great quantities. Containers, alas, were not. Applicants should be urged to bring their own boxes, baskets, pails, envelopes, etc.

Next came the staff shortages in Africa. People might walk fifty miles to the nearest Dispensary, only to find it closed. Perhaps the overworked official had collapsed with fever, perhaps he had gone AWOL, or deserted, or been murdered by black-marketeers. No one knew. Angry crowds began burning Dispensaries, not only in Africa but across the world. Officials now began to desert in greater numbers, or call for military protection.

At the end of a year, the League reviewed its campaign: The costs (of troops, compensation for riot-torn cities, etc.) ran to billions. The results were disappointing. Fewer than a tenth of those in need had actually been reached.

Reluctantly, the League voted to dispense no more boxes of God.

Assessment

Our machine slaves have now taken over all tedious or disagreeable occupations. They paint, write and perform music, make scientific discoveries, and handle pretty well everything from fashion to philosophy. This leaves us plenty of time and freedom to do whatever we like – extract square roots, say, or calculate payrolls.

Art News

Sisyphus jammed a block of wood under the stone to keep it

from rolling back, took a swig from his canteen, and squatted down to explain his work to the tour group.

'Of course, it's a very healthy life – outdoor work, and so on. Then, too, I've always liked working with natural materials like stone. Not that the stone itself is important. No, what's important here is not gross physical change. I think I can safely say that ever since Oldenburg dug a hole in Central Park, filled it in, and called it a buried sculpture – ever since then, physical-change stuff has been dying a slow death. Nowadays, the artist is not concerned with torturing Nature to "make" something. He's concerned with "doing" something *within* Nature . . .'

After stopping for ice-cold orangeade, the group moved on to Tantalus.

Pax Gurney

As a young man, Gurney said, 'If I were world emperor, the first thing I'd do would be to introduce a compulsory world language.' For the next twenty years, he actually worked on such a language, Unilingo, on the off chance he might become emperor. Unilingo was designed to guarantee world peace forever. In this language, no one could lie or express hatred or discontent. No one could hold an opinion contrary to fact, or hold any opinion at all about non-facts. No two speakers of Unilingo could ever really disagree. Gurney described it in his memoirs as 'a calculus of good sense and good taste'.

Of course he *did* become world emperor, and the world prospered for many years under his 'rule of grammar'. People stopped talking about matters that did not concern them, and spoke wisely of those that did. The world was at peace. Gurney abdicated, and the institutions of government withered as people learned self-control.

A century after Gurney's death, an American compiling a new dictionary of Unilingo made a curious discovery. While in America the word *orth* had kept its original meaning ('to fray the edge of an old blanket, from left to right'), in Eurasiafrica it had taken on a new one ('to fray the edge of an old blanket, left-handedly'). He wrote a letter about it to a Eurasiafrican colleague. The trouble was traced to photocopies of Gurney's original manuscript, on file in the two continents. One copy showed the word *riin* ('from left to right'), the other showed *rïin* without a dot over the second *i* ('left-handedly'). An interesting dispute arose between the Universities of Tübingen and Nebraska.

What had been on the original manuscript (long since lost)? Was a dot added, correcting a mistake? Or erased? Was the addition or erasure itself a mistake? Physical chemists were called in, and photography experts. The debate became more heated, and opinions were split along continental lines. An American professor was booed at Tübingen; Nebraska fired a foreign archaeologist.

Over the next century, the two continents grew apart. The dot-less Eurasiafricans developed a philosophy aimed at defining the final meaning of life. The dotted Americans preferred a harsh form of skepticism, summed up in their motto: 'That which does not exist is nonexistent.' Two centuries later, these philosophies had become articles of faith for two bitterly opposed religions.

Knowing this background to the present war, we can more easily understand . . .

A Fable

The snails, discontented with their free and easy life, held a noisy meeting to petition Jupiter for a king.

'We're not complaining,' they insisted. 'We know we already have portable homes and other luxuries. But we'd like a strong leader. After all, you gave the frogs a stork to follow. And even the men have their presidents. How about us?'

Jupiter threw an old log down into their pool and said, 'There is a king for you!'

The old log has proved a wise and compassionate leader. Under his guidance, the snails have prospered, until now they are seen in all the best restaurants.

Utopia: A Financial Report

Utopia is laid out in four planned nations: Fascesia, Commund, Capitalia, and Anarche.

Fascesia is a half-tamed land. The cities are sophisticated, filled with monumental architecture, opera houses, and elegant night clubs. The countryside, on the other hand, is a wilderness teeming (in theory) with savages and wild game. Alas, Fascesians tend to hunt both to extinction, and the cost of replenishing these is considerable. Therefore we recommend closing Fascesia.

Commund cities are bleak and industrial, while its rural areas undergo intensive agriculture. Communders are excellent organizers and produce surpluses yearly. Unfortunately, these surpluses seem to lower the morale of Communders, who rather enjoy mild discomforts and privations – proof that they are continuing their 'struggle'. Accordingly, we remove their surpluses from time to time, as well as causing them to have minor shortages. The costs of removal and destruction of their surpluses have become excessive. Moreover, the materials destroyed are our loss, in the last analysis. We recommend closing Commund.

Capitalia is a uniformly settled nation with a monotony of maple-lined streets and white frame houses. Capitalians have no incentive to work (though of course they refer to their play activities as 'work'; e.g. signing their names to pieces of paper). They also require huge outlays of energy, materials, machines, foods, and medicines. We recommend closing Capitalia.

Anarche seemed at first a viable nation, with few requirements. Now it is entirely deserted. Anarchers are evidently unstable, and frequently migrate to the other three nations.

Summary: We feel the experiment has served its purpose. We now know more than enough about the social institutions of *Homo sapiens*. We feel, therefore, that Utopia should be closed and its inhabitants destroyed. The ground can then be used for a study of the social behavior of another interesting species, the armadillos.

Utopiary

Utopia has turned out to be like a well-planned garden: Each change of season brings its fresh cycle of pleasing color, heavenly scent, and backbreaking work.

Luck

General Holme threw the dice. 'Tough luck, General Vladiful,' he said, chuckling. 'I've just captured your fourth army. Do you want to surrender?'

The other sighed. 'No, no. After all, we are playing for real armies. Let us play on awhile. I may yet turn the turtles on you, eh?'

'Tables. We say turn the tables. Ha-ha, I must say, this beats the old system of waging w—'

The door burst open and a soldier strode in, pointing a submachine gun at them. 'You'll have to surrender. This sector has just been captured by the forces of General Heinz.'

'Heinz? Heinz?' Holme scratched his head. 'Never heard of him. He's not in the game.'

'He plays a bigger game,' said the soldier. 'Come with me, please.'

Vladiful nodded. 'So, there is a bigger war than we know of, even. I wonder who Heinz opposes?'

From the darkness outside came a burst of automatic fire. The soldier flopped to the floor, bleeding from a dozen wounds. In a moment, a man in a Germanic uniform was prodded into the room at bayonet point.

'I am Heinz,' he said. 'Are you my captors?'

'Not us.' Holme offered him some brandy. 'Ask the man with the gun.'

The man with the gun cleared his throat. 'This sector – namely, Earth – has just been captured by Planet Marshal Gordon. You are all under house arrest.'

As if echoing him, an amplified voice rolled over the dark parade ground outside. 'You are all under house arrest. This sector has just been captured by the 119th Galactic Army under Commander Noll.'

'Noll?' said Holme. 'Lucky bastard. I wonder what *he* threw.'

A Picnic

Bill Nolan was thinking out loud. 'In a way, I guess this *is* Utopia. I mean, people in the past would have been horrified at the idea of having a picnic in a junkyard. They weren't like us.'

Jimmy stopped kicking at an old tire. 'Why, Dad?'

Nolan rescued the baby, who was crawling around elbow-deep in sump oil. 'That's enough, hon. Mommy'll bring your bottle in just a minute.' He waved to his wife, who was climbing over a crumpled Buick.

'You see, Jimmy, our stomachs are different. Everybody has a lot of little helpers in his stomach, to help him digest his dinner. But the way it used to be, the helpers couldn't handle much of anything. So people had to eat things like – oh, cows, pigs, and so on.'

Jimmy looked up at him. 'Cows! No kidding?'

'I used to eat pieces of cow myself. (Hey, did you strip that insulation like your mother said? Good boy.) No, what happened was, some scientists changed the little helpers. See, we were running out of cows and stuff, so we needed helpers that would help us eat new things. Now just about everything is edible.'

'You're not supposed to say "et".'

'Yes, but "edible" means "eatable". I used to wonder why myself.'

'Mumf chmumf—'

'Don't let your mother see you talking with your mouth full, son.'

Janet Nolan came back to the picnic site just then. 'See what? Oh, God, Bill, you let the baby get herself *filthy*. Couldn't you have spooned up the sump oil instead of letting her crawl right in it? And, Jimmy! What are you doing?'

A large piece of the old tyre was gone, and the boy was now swallowing a strip of muddy tread.

'I was hungry,' he mumbled.

'Hungry? That's no excuse for bolting your food. You'll have a tummy ache.'

'Stomach,' the boy corrected.

'I don't see why boys who bolt their food should have any dessert, do you? And we're having polyethylene seat covers.'

'Aw, Ma, can't I have some?'

'Hmm. We'll see.'

Bill looked at the baby's bottle in her hand. 'I see you got it.'

She smiled. 'Yes. Real high-octane lead-free stuff. Only a little rusty water in the bottom. We were lucky to find it, she's so fussy.'

Janet delivered the bottle into the frantically waving arms of the baby, who rammed it in her own mouth and started sucking. Long before the others had finished twirling up masses of plastic wire insulation on their forks, the bottle was empty. The baby lay back, flushed and drowsy. Nolan gave her a cardboard cookie, but, after slobbering at it for a moment without really biting it, she gave an aromatic burp and went to sleep.

'Utopia,' he murmured.

'What, darling?'

'Nothing.' He brandished the carving knife and fork. 'Now for the main course. White sidewall, darling? Or dark?'

Scenes from Rural Life

The sound of a horse and wagon moving down the street penetrated to the lounge bar. Two fat men sat at a table listening.

'Nice, that,' said the younger reporter. 'The sound of an uneaten horse.'

The older reporter removed his clay pipe. 'O thou cynical young man. Soon you'll get disillusioned with cynicism, and then what?' He twiddled his empty glass, calling attention to it.

'Same again, Peter?'

When the young reporter came back with the drinks, he stopped to stare at himself in the mirror behind their table. The mirror advertised a beer that KEEPS YOU FIT. His face fit into the decorative letters, so that YOU sat upon his forehead and his beard was twined with gilt sheaves of grain.

'Cheers. Harry's promised to join us later. You won't remember Harry. Before your time, Elvis.'

'I remember him. There's a stud missing off my hatband.' Elvis took off his sombrero and examined it. 'Christ, here's another.'

'Cheap Albanian goods,' said Peter. 'Or wherever they make them. What you want is a worry-hat. I'm a-fixing to get me one next month.' He showed the younger man a tattered brochure. Worry-hats were handsome sombreros that grew more handsome with wear. The felt was impregnated with a silicone substance that resisted sweat and hair-oil, leaving a dry design in the usual dark stain.

'Good old Harry's gone and got one already. Harry always had all the answers first. You know, he scooped the Miss World kidnapping.'

'Miss World?'

'Before your time, son. Those were the days. Before everybody got fat on peanut oil and – do I hear rain out there?'

'No.'

The door opened and a young woman came in, shaking her umbrella. She started for the bar, then swerved and came over to their table.

'Hi, I'm Sue Stiles. *Harrow Express*. You must be Pete and Elve.'

Peter Fry and Elvis Dinsdale introduced themselves, and Elvis offered to buy her a drink.

'Can't, they don't serve women here. Anyway, we ought to be across the street. They're coming any minute now.'

'We're waiting for a mate.'

'Harry Sheppard? He's not coming. I'm covering the conference for him.'

Peter threaded the pipestem through slits in his hat, pinning the brim back. 'Not coming? A conference of world economic advisers, the most important ever, and Harry can't make it?'

Elvis winked. 'Maybe he's scooping his own kidnapping?'

Jeannie thought she would remember this day as long as she lived. The customer's crazy, dangerous grin – his wild eyes – could this be happening? Even his strange request?

'I want to draw ten pounds, please,' he said.

Her first impulse was to pull the alarm string that would jingle a cowbell outside the bank door. But she could imagine blue-eyed Constable Higgins laughing at her fears. *Keep calm, Jeannie*, she told herself.

'Do you have an account here? Sir?'

'Of course I have an account here. And it is from that very account that I want to draw ten pounds. If you please.'

'I'm afraid you'll have to see the manager. Won't keep you a minute.'

She nodded at Jack, who had heard it all. He capped his 'fountain' pen. After the gaze of his steel-grey eyes had swept the customer, memorizing his features, he went up to fetch Mr Selly.

In a moment the manager came striding down the stairs, followed by the billows of his smock. His grin looked a bit scared.

'Well, well, Mr Cutler, is it? No? Ah, no matter. So you want to draw out all your funds, do you?'

'No, just ten pounds. What's the fuss about? I mean.'

'Ha ha, yes, I see. Your money after all. But you will understand that this is just a bit irregular. Have you made an arrangement to draw?'

'I didn't know I had to do that.'

'Well, you don't, of course. But it's usual. You see, we're not really equipped to deal with a sudden large withdrawal. Now the question is, mm—' Mr Selly pushed back his straw hat and scratched at a scab high up his forehead. 'The question is, what do you want it for? I can't believe you're dissatisfied with our interest rates. National Westmidland Barcminster pay the highest possible return on your capital. You won't do better elsewhere, you know. The Squatters Building Society pay only eighteen per cent – and anyway, we're just completing negotiations to take them over. Were you thinking of buying something? Because you know we have easy terms for scrip loans. But your *money* is far better off where it is now.'

'That may be, but I want to draw ten pounds. I didn't think—'

'Nor should you.' Mr Selly jumped up and sat on the narrow counter, dangling his legs. '*Don't* think, I implore you. That's our job, *thinking money*. We could invest your savings for you. We know all about shares. Labour camps, disaster area finance, council housing, rollsroycettes – every aspect. You can hear our investment computer right now in the back room, clattering out the answers. Stalk?'

Mr Selly produced two haystalks and offered him one. 'No? I hope you don't mind if I indulge.' He unwrapped one and put it between his teeth. 'Helps pass the time. Yes. Helps pass the – well, I've enjoyed our little chat.' He jumped down and shook hands with the customer, murmuring what might have been his name. 'Feel free to drop in again, anytime. I like to think of our branch as a little – supermarket – you know, where all our friends can drop in anytime for a good natter. I believe that's the word.'

The man started shouting about his ten pounds, saying he'd walked fifty miles across London to get here.

'Look,' he said. 'Is it a question of identification or something?'

'No, no, of course not. We're not like the Post Office, fingerprints and all that. Your face is all the identification you ever need with us.'

'Well then just give me the money.'

'Hmm. A lot of money to carry about, isn't it, sir?'

'If I'm not worried, why should you be? What is it, in the vault or something? A time lock? Why are you stalling?'

'Stalling? Not at all. Ha ha, the fact is, we don't have it here at all.'

'A bank without money?'

'We're only a small branch.'

'A bank without m— and you call your adding machine a computer – I've heard bloody everything now.' The customer did a little shuffling dance. Jeannie saw he would hit Mr Selly if someone didn't do something.

'We could give you a *post-dated* scrip,' she suggested. 'Then you could spend it whenever you liked.'

'I don't want *scrip*. I want a nice new ten-pound note with the King's picture on it. I want a real banknote in my hands.'

Mr Selly's shoulders drooped from 9.15 to 8.20. 'Yes, I see. Very well, you shall have it. But there are a few formalities, you understand. Jeannie, will you and Jack take care of this *customer*?'

Jack asked him the questions for the form, while Jeannie wheeled over to the phone and dialled the number of the Secpol Agency.

'Tea,' said the voice on the line.

Jeannie ran her finger down the day-code sheet. 'Milk and sugar,' she replied. 'Three lumps.'

'Oh, hello, Jeannie. What is it this time? A transfer?'

'Use the code,' she said crossly. 'Are you ready?'

'Ready.'

'Edna's force parts wishbone buzz three. Buzz buzz two, Everest dingy omelette. How far? Portage seventeen nought wedding cake.' Her legs ached, as they always did when things were upsetting. 'Coffee.'

'Coffee.' The voice read back her message. 'Seventeen nought wedding cake? Jesus, that comes to ten knicker. Is it a run on the bank?'

'Coffee and cream,' she said firmly and hung up. What was the use of even having a code if someone was going to spell it out like that? Anyone might be listening. Banks were supposed to represent security, for heaven's sake.

'Any identifying scars?' said Jack. 'Any birthmarks or tattoos?'

'Are you a newpaper man?'
'No, I'm a real man.'

–*Chafed Elbows*

The newsmen were sheltering in the lobby. As the time of arrival approached, they began to bunch together near the door, so closepacked that the microphone of A was entangled with the fringe on B's leather-style jacket, while C's sombrero was knocked to the floor by D, as he craned over E's shoulder. F trampled on the hat while trying to get his camera clear of G's knapsack and blanket roll. E was leaning at a funny angle, having already found out that every time H sneezed, whoever was behind him got spurred.

Outside it was raining and would rain again. Other men set up tripods on the wet grass of the street, aiming their cameras at the place where the official rollsroycettes would stop.

Prof. Dr Schollfuss of East Germany came first. His sleek machine pulled up and, while the driver tried to look more arrogant and less wet and exhausted, Dr Schollfuss explained to the newsmen that he had no comment to make at this time. The situation was grave, but this conference could, as they said, produce a lasting solution.

'Currency reform?'

'Certainly currency reform,' he said, hefting a large suitcase from the roof of his vehicle. 'But what kind, and how – how extensive, is too early to say. We hope. We hope.'

The American and Tunisian economists arrived together, and had no comment to make. The Mexican expert took a pessimistic view, but hoped that export balance agreements would be the main area of improvement. None of the others had anything to say, and the reporters taped it all.

'Our own finance minister, Mr Norman Coutts, looked fit for the inevitable battle at the conference table,' reporter E later wrote. 'Like the others, Mr Coutts wore the traditional black cut-away coat and striped trousers, but relieved the sombre tone by adding a bright yellow tea-rose to his buttonhole. Thus Britain brings to the table at least the appearance of hope.'

Better not to mention that the minister had also inked his ankle to hide a few sock-holes, thought E. Searching for a punch line, he scratched at the spur marks on his own ankle.

'But is a brave front enough?'

'But it isn't a question of class war at all,' Mrs Fordyce was trying to say. 'This is a threat the whole community must meet.'

What was the point? If even Prouty, with his bullhorn voice and a face that reminded Mrs Fordyce of the young Uncle Sam, if even he couldn't get through, how could she hope to make them hear over their own shouting?

'Who gets the benefit, that's all I want to know. Who . . .'

'You just try telling *that* to . . .'

'. . . the point anyway. The revolution . . .'

'Listen. Just listen a minute. We . . .'

'. . . our fucking priorities!'

'. . . tricity Board. And if the troops . . .'

'. . . Action Committee, not some bloody Fine Arts Apprec . . .'

'LISTEN!' Prouty shouted.

'. . . to have a plan,' finished Zero.

Prouty wasn't tall, but when he stood up on the bale-of-hay sofa to address them, his US face looked down from near the ceiling. 'Listen, I know you're all excited, but we agreed to do this thing quietly. If you all go belting out of here like a pack of drunks, we won't make it to the end of the street, let alone Forage Park. And – Colonel, will you shut up and listen? – and I want all those axes out of sight. Zero's got the idea.'

Zero Young showed them how to hook the axeblade in the armhole of an overcoat. The women were to carry coils of rope and tins of paraffin in their egg-basket handbags. Mrs Fordyce stopped listening. All she could think of was this wretched little flat. How could Mr Prouty stand living here, cramped up in what they called a council ranch?

'I'm so nervous,' said Clara Bond. 'What if we get caught? What if my boss finds out?'

The Colonel patted her arm.

Prouty said, 'We'd better leave in two's and three's. Meet at the generating station in five minutes.'

The Stoddard boy laughed. 'What generating station?'

For some reason – perhaps because he worked in a plas-timber yard, or went around with his mouth open – the Stoddard boy had a reputation for wit. Now everyone laughed with him but Clara. She went off to find Prouty's toilet.

He stepped down from the sofa and clapped his hands. 'Right then, let's go.'

'What about Clara?'

'She's to stay here and phone the newspaper.'

Stoddard made some remark about paper and they set off.

'Fertilizer,' said Harry Sheppard.

Sue looked up from her conference story. 'I beg your pardon?'

'Fertilizer. I've been over every clipping for ten years back. There has to be some connection between phantom riots and fertilizer.'

'Think I should mention the minister's inked ankle?'

He slapped his desk and stood up. 'You write your story and I'll write mine.'

'Where are you going?'

'To the pictures. I think better under sedation.'

The grazing park, once they were inside, seemed bigger and blacker than they'd imagined. Mrs Fordyce insisted they were heading in the wrong direction.

'I don't remember all those clumps of bushes,' she said, pointing a finger no one could see at the darker smudges on the hillside.

'No, we're right.' The Colonel went forward. In nights he could remember, the sky here would have shown the yellow glow of London, and the objective would be a clear silhouette against it. Curious. Because of course the tower wouldn't have been there then, not with the lights. The field and figure occupied entirely different universes, as it were. This tower: therefore, no street lamps.

The clumps of bushes, as they drew nearer, became sleeping cows. They stirred, lowing, and moved off downhill when the noise of chopping began.

Clara was unable to flush the toilet, there being no used dishwater left in Prouty's bucket. She threw open his front window and breathed in the cleansing air. No smell, no stain. From the hill came faint echoing raps.

Prouty had left the warning and phone number next to the phone. Clara picked up the paper – a leaf from some old paperback – and rehearsed the message:

'We, the Action Committee of Concerned Individuals to Disrupt Electrical Nuisance Towers, are calling to tell you we've just pulled down and burnt the generating plant in Forage Park. Let this be a warning to the Electricity Board. If they think they can put a dangerous windmill right here, where it could blow down and electrocute us and our children, let them beware. We will destroy every windmill they build. We will put a stop to these dangerous and senseless experiments. This is only the beginning.'

Norman Coutts pulled the wilted rose from his buttonhole and flung it on the table.

'It's all a waste of time,' he said. 'Gentlemen, can't we at least agree to give the afrodollar a crawling peg? What else are we here for?'

'Look, Norman. Think a minute.' Happy Schine of the USA opened a folder. 'You know it's suicide for the escudo. And you may or may not agree that the escudo is just about the most contagious currency in the bloc.'

The man from Senegal shook his head. 'We're going at this from the wrong end. Why not begin with the Rio conference dollar. That's the source of the epidemic. You all assume we're going to keep bailing it out forever, and that's not realistic.'

'The Rio dollar is alive and well and living in Argentina,' said the Saudi. 'But look what it's resting on – a god-damned platform of rotten schillings!'

'I'm going to bed,' said Coutts. 'We're bound to see this in a different light tomorrow.' As he left the room, all the lights went out.

'There's Britain for you,' said the Korean's voice. 'They want to manage everyone's economy, while at home they have a strike every five minutes.'

'Throughout the world, grass provides food, both grain and meat, heat, shelter, clothing, weapons and tools, drugs and herbs, and of course life-giving oxygen. We may indeed say with the poet, "All flesh is grass".'

—Lord Spoggett, chairman, Plastics Board. The girl ahead of Biron kept getting winks and grins from the young sergeant behind the counter.

'I'm sorry, miss, but if he's not a relative, we can't look for Mr Sheppard, unless we have reason to suspect a crime has been committed.'

'Yes, but can't you—?'

'There's nothing stopping you from going to Secpol, of course. I understand their rates are very reasonable.'

His face was sunburned and his straw-coloured hair damp, as though he'd just rushed in from the plough to deal out police advice. He saluted as Biron stepped up.

'Yes sir?'

'My name is Biron Johnson.'

Ignoring the noise from the next room, the sergeant carefully entered this on a form.

'My parents are missing. Carl and Helen Johnson. And my sister Carolinda.' Their names were taken down.

'Yes sir. Now your address?' Next door, something thumped against the wall a few times.

'Well, we don't exactly have an address as yet. We'd only just got to London, to look for work.'

'I see. This does make a problem. If we locate them, how can we get in touch—?'

'Griffiths!' someone shouted next door.

'Excuse me, sir.' The sergeant took a length of iron pipe from under the counter and went next door. Now Biron noticed that his uniform was completed with jeans and worn carpet slippers.

In a few minutes he came back, smoothing his hair. 'The best thing,' he panted, 'the best thing would be for you to get yourself a fixed address. Until then, you'd best drop in to see us once a week. Friday mornings are reporting days. And – oh, where did you last see your family?'

'In a cinema queue in the West End.'

'All-night cinema was it? *Dossarama*? Happens all the time. I imagine they've just ditched you, lad.'

Biron stared up for a moment at a yellow poster: FREE FOOD WITH THE METROPOLITAN POLICE.

'Well. I'll check back then, Friday morning.'

'You'd better.'

'That's where I want to go, I want to stay,
In Tanzy,

Tanzy,
In Tanzy far away.'

– work song

'I know it's a local story,' Elvis said. 'But it's news. I mean, the first mugging for real money in London, in – years and years. Ten quid!'

'The sub won't buy it,' said Peter. 'How can he? The last story we printed about Secpol brought a writ.'

'But they were only dressed like men of the Security Police Agency. That's not libel.'

'It is now; we can't mention their name. You want something to do? I'll give you something to do. Write up a little story about Harry Sheppard's disppearance.'

'I am, I am. Peter, I talked to Sue Stiles. She said he left the office raving about horse shit.'

That afternoon, Norman Coutts conceded that Britain might accept a gold graft scheme, provided the Hungarian loan could be buried. Jesus Figueras of Venezuela made a counter-proposal: nail the Hungarian loan to the Rio dollar float, and buy off the exchange surplus with dirhan. Evan MacIntyre of Canada thought this might be more stable if run in tandem with a limited-access overdraft agreement between the USSR and Rhodesia, monitored by the UAR.

The UAR economist said he had a headache, and was going for an afternoon nap.

Father Millennium wanted them all to understand the need for a careful study of the Mysteries. Did anyone here know the Welsh were descended from space travellers? That duplicates of Stonehenge had been found on the Moon, only the authorities wouldn't release the photos? We were, he said, being lied to by those in power.

Shading his eyes from the sun, Biron lay back in the grass and listened to the frail voice. A bird squawked somewhere, just once. He dozed, dreaming of a dark, narrow street. A huge shape came rushing towards him, about to crush him against the wall.

Was it a wagon? He couldn't remember. It vanished like the taste of the 'soup'.

Sue Stiles copied all the notes from Harry Sheppard's desk into a list:

tooth house
phantom riot (s)
phone Briggs for council mins
fertiliser grows!!!
import statistics√
farms how deliver?
whose???
check D-notice applics
cartoon: the lost chord? (crossed out)

MI5	10	11	9	13	13
MI6	4	2	–	6	1
Metpol	49	58	43	48	61
Secpol	18	21	34	56	111

seated one day at the organ . . .

The list made no sense. Every item was either banal or surreal. She spent an afternoon finding out that the numbers meant applications for D-notices over the past five years, then she tore up the list and forgot about it, or nearly.

Next day the tooth story broke.

The smell of eggs frying in butter drifted out the kitchen door of the farmhouse. Carolinda and her new friend hurried towards it, carrying a pail between them.

'Don't let any flies in,' said the farmer's wife. 'Hungry, girls?'

They nodded.

'Yes, the new prisoners always are. Be ready in a minute, dears. Cut yourselves some bread. I can't fuss with toast, but I always like to give my girls a decent breakfast. You won't find it hard work here, whatever they say about labour camps. We expect a full day's work for a full day's food, mind, but that's all. Not like some camps I could mention. What's up, girl? Sorry for your sins?'

'I was just wondering about my parents,' said Carolinda. 'They were arrested with me. Do you think they might be on a good farm like this? And my brother Biron.'

'They might even be here, my dear. It's a big farm. Let's see: you give me their names, and I'll ask Rufus. He keeps the books. And don't you be afraid of Rufus, neither of you. He almost never uses the whip, I'll say that. He curses, but he's a fair man.'

Carolinda's new friend, Clara, asked to be excused, to go to the toilet.

By 4 a.m. there were only three men left at the conference table. Hap Schine (USA), Alonzo Tomas (Spain) and Kai Sung (China). The others had drifted off to the dormitory.

Hap chewed a blade of cuticle off his finger and spat it out. 'Okay, why don't we play it this way: Peg the zloty against the escudo, float it against the dirhan, and let the rand and ruble find their own level against a modified float of all three. When—'

Sung shook his head. 'You've forgotten—'

'Lemme finish, will you? *When* that level is ahead of the Israeli pound parity float, we get a new flow of pesetas to balance the transfer of pesos and duros. Am I right or wrong?'

'Well, right in theory, but—'

'Okay, listen. When that happens, we pump the brakes a little by a schilling leak. Now the afrodollar—'

'Happy, Happy, you're forgetting about three things. We have to balance the peseta flow by a quick transfer of ticals to Hungary *and* by—'

'Hold it.' Hap spoke to the servant who had just entered. 'Charles, can you get us some sandwiches and coffee – no, make it tea.'

'I'm sorry, sir.'

'What for?'

'I'm sorry, sir. We have orders. The conference credit was suspended at midnight.'

'Oh, Jesus, did you hear that? Welcome to Britain. They can't even afford to feed us. Look Charles, take my goddamned watch.'

'Don't be a child,' said Alonzo. 'That's a gold watch, Happy.'

'Yeah, but it doesn't taste too good. You got a better idea?'

'Yes I have. We each brought things to use for spending money outside, did we not? I brought cigars, Sung brought cotton clothes, and so on. You must have something like that.'

'Cigarettes, but they're in the dorm.'

'Charles will take our notes, will he not?'

Charles would. For twenty long cigarettes, two cigars, and two cotton shirts, he would bring six ham sandwiches and one and a half litres of tea.

'Now where were we? Look, Sung, I know all about the forty per cent discount on drachmas in Paraguay. But if we get India and Uruguay to . . .'

The card in the newsagent's window said: 'Young men and women wanted for interesting work, exchangeable vouchers. Short evening hours. Must be in *perfect* physical condition.'

The youth in the surgical collar next to Biron watched him reading it. 'Stay clear of that one. Bus conducting. Has to be.'

'Clipping tickets or something?'

'Clipping tickets? You must be from the Moon. Man, bus conductors *pull the buses*. You know how heavy a bus is?'

Biron had a hard time believing stories like that. Londoners were always joking. Surely they had horses for pulling? Anyway, he hadn't seen a bus since he'd arrived.

'I think I'll risk it.'

'You'll see. Buses. Or else foodfactory. That's nasty, food-factory. You think at least you'll get a meal, but they never feed you what they make. I worked six months in a pork pie factory, and the only pork you ever see is on the assembly line. Fibre, that's what they gave us.'

The address on the card was the top floor of a tall office block in Soholborn. Biron sat in a pleasant, beige waiting room with a few dozen other men and one woman. A secretary came in and ordered them to take off their shoes and walk up and down. A man missing a thumb was dismissed. The secretary told the others they'd be given a bath and enough clothes to make them presentable. 'Can you all dance? Anyone who can't?'

Biron put up his hand.

'Well, never mind, you can stumble about. They don't expect much.'

'They?'

'The clients. Good grief, didn't you all see Mr Bowder? No? Oh. Well, you're all dates for our computer party. The clients are to think you're all randomly selected dates, just like them. So don't tell them you work here, or you're out.

'Now. We provide food and one drink. Anything extra comes out of your vouchers. Understood?'

Biron managed it well enough. When a girl in a wheelchair (all the clients seemed to be handicapped) asked him to dance, he didn't know exactly what she meant. She explained finally that he was just to sort of wheel her back and forth in time to the music.

At Euston Station, Biron sat in the little chair attached to the television set and dropped in his token. The screen instantly showed men with briefcases getting out of their pedal cars and entering a building.

'. . . arrived here two days ago seeking a solution to the afro-dollar currency crisis. An interim report issued today said that a tentative solution is in the offing. Nevertheless, it added, the world currency situation will remain shaky for some time to come. No doubt the escudo will eventually be revalued, despite the hardship this may mean to importers of synthetic port.'

Without pictures, the news reader said, 'The Home Office tonight denied rumours of a large riot yesterday in a London suburb. There had been a small disturbance outside the "Hay Wain" public house, nothing more. Earlier reports of fifty policemen injured were exaggerated. The private Security Police Agency confirmed the Home Office statement.

'In the Commons, the Prime Minister issued a denial today of the rumoured bomb at Number Ten this morning. A fire marshall had already confirmed the official explanation of a gas leak in the central heating system. The entire system is to be checked for further flaws, and the Prime Minister said he now considered the matter closed.

'A Parliamentary enquiry has been called for by the shadow Housing Minister, to look into alleged breaches of Public Health regulations in council dwellings.'

Another speaker came on the screen. 'The row grew up over the use of building materials from graveyards, a practice allowed in certain cases, but not generally known to the public. Last week, two children playing about the tip of rubble being prepared for concrete mixing on a North London ranch estate, found these objects, now known to be human bones.'

The screen showed teeth and jagged lumps. 'Regulations permit the use of bones only from graves more than fifty years old. But some experts say these bones are perhaps as recent as a year old. How did they get into the mix? I asked the estate building materials manager, Gerard Hollis.'

A man in a chrome helmet said he had no comment at this stage.

'But surely, Mr Hollis, you have some idea where these came from?'

'Aye.'

'Some people are shocked by the idea of using graveyard materials at all. Have you anything to say to them?'

'Aye, they don't ask, do they? Where their houses come from. They just ask for more and more houses.'

'Do you know which graveyards have been quarried?'

'No, I don't. I never heard of any being dug into, not for ten years. But the bones keep turnin' up. All the men know it, like. What can we do? We don't use naught that's useful to nobody.'

'Doesn't grave-robbing bother—'

'I've as much respect as any man for the dead. But I think of the living first. That's how I see it.'

Another face came on the screen. 'We'll be back after a short break with more news of the King's visit to a labour camp, cricket test results, and why this vintage pop-up toaster fetched seventy thousand pounds at Sotheby's.'

Two women appeared in a supermarket. Aloud, one thought, 'How does she make her scrip vouchers go so far? I can never afford to give my Ernie meat more than twice a week. And he won't touch these meat substitutes.' The camera closed in on a box the other woman was taking from a shelf. 'Drew's Ready Lamb? Well I'll be – dried substitute that's been stewed in real lamb juices. Hmm. I wonder if Ernie would like it?'

She was about to serve it to Ernie when Biron's machine clicked off. An old man in town clothes nudged him.

'You should have watched the other side. They never show food on the other side. Better not to stare at the food, eh? Give us a token, will you?'

Biron gave him his last token. 'Not much use to me, anyway. I have to get my train back to the inn now, and scrip's no good tomorrow.'

'There's never a cop around when you need one.'

– old saying

Captain Grayson was just saying over the phone, 'They've done it this time. What? Yes. Only grabbed a fucking reporter with their fucking snatch squad, that's all. We'll cover it, but it stinks.'

Hap Schine had just won all of Alonzo Tomas's cigars at Monopoly. Carolinda was writing down the names of her parents for the farmer's wife. Peter Fry was looking for his thesaurus. Mrs Fordyce was answering the door. The Prime Minister was trying to telephone Captain Grayson of the Secpol Agency. Prouty was answering the door. Clara Bond was turning a crank to crush milky juice out of a plant. Zero Young was answering the door. The Stoddard boy, his mouth open, was answering the door.

On the dark train, Biron stared out at more darkness. Probably Mum and Dad and Carolinda had left London altogether. Too confusing and tense here, anyway. Why stick around. There were jobs going in Tanzania . . .

What was England, anyway? Grass, that's all. A lot of cheap green grass, eventually it goes brown and it's hay, and . . .

There weren't any women, for one thing. Where were all the women? Just a few cripples left. And no jobs and no money and no houses. They pretend it's all a farm, but you never see anyone ploughing a field or anything. And cows. Where did they keep the cows? Just a few in the park for show. Were the women all out milking the cows or what?

The lights came on suddenly. A man stood in the aisle, struggling with two men in green helmets and uniforms. A woman screamed.

'It's a mistake,' the man shouted. 'I was just giving her back her handbag.'

'In the dark?' One Secpol man hit him in the face and throat until he fell, scattering a handful of scrip notes.

The little old man in a gray cap waited until they had dragged away the thief in handcuffs. Then he moved down the aisle, clipping tickets.

'Where would we be without them?' he said, over and over.

Biron surrendered his ticket.

'This is yesterday's. No good.'

'It can't be! I just bought it at the window!'

'Don't try that, son. Show me a proper ticket. Do you have one?'

'No, but I'll pay—'

'Guards!'

One of the security policemen came running, drawing his cosh.

'Here's one for you. Fake ticket.'

'I'm willing to pay—'

The guard hit him in the shoulder, not viciously but as if testing his solidity. Biron's arm went numb.

The old man cackled. 'They're always willing to pay, once they know what's coming.'

The Secpol man dragged Biron to the end seat and handcuffed him to the baggage rack, so that he had to sit with his numb arm suspended above him. The thief sat opposite, and a man in green sat next to each prisoner.

When they lifted their face shields, the Secpol men didn't look menacing any more. The young one beside Biron had effeminate features (for a wild moment Biron thought he knew where all the women were) and the old one had acne scars.

'What happens to me now?'

The young one smiled. 'You'll see. You'll know the difference.'

But the older one stopped licking a hand-rolled cigarette and shook his head. 'Not to worry,' he said. 'You should get off light. Month in labour camp. We won't say anything about resisting arrest, lad. If you stay easy.'

Biron felt better at once. As the train finished its run and went into a long shed, he slipped into his daydream: row on row of cows with milkmaids pumping at their bellies, filling the blue pails. Just as one of the milkmaids turned to smile at him, the younger guard stabbed Biron through his dreaming eye.

The fertilizer man's great wagon was waiting by the depot door. While the younger man humped the two bodies over, the older one counted the eggs.

'Not enough, Rufus. God damn me, but I told you last night, we want fourteen eggs for each lump.'

'Next time, maybe. I don't need your lot, you know. I got me enough here already. Been to a bombing and a riot. Tomorrow night I got a load of anarchists coming. Them what burned up the windmill, is who.' He took the identity papers of Biron and the other, marking them in his book as bomb victims. The Secpol men gave a push, helping his mules start up the great creaking wagon.

Rufus tore a big piece of bread and mopped up the egg from his plate. 'Johnson? Had a few of them lately. One young fellow last night, as I recall. Now let me see, three days ago . . .'

His thumb left grease-prints on the ledger sheets as he turned them. On the radio a bull was lowing. 'Yes, here they are. Fertilizer, both of 'em. Or so I tell the busybodies down at the Town Hall.' He snapped the ledger shut and went on eating.

'Anyway, it's none of their business, what I feed my pigs and chickens. They're always glad to get the bones, for their darned houses. Any more bacon going, Margaret?'

'Cheerio, Mrs Archer,' said a voice on the radio.

'Cheerio, Tom.'

The Secret of the Old Custard

Agnes had been wishing for a baby all day, so it was no surprise to her when she peeked through the glass door of the oven and found one. Bundled in clean flannel, it slept on the wire rack while she scrubbed out dusty bottles, fixed formula and dragged down the crib from the attic. By the time Glen came home from work, she was giving the baby its first bottle.

'Look!' she exclaimed. 'A baby!'

'O my God, where did you get that?' he said, his healthy pink face going white. 'You know it's illegal to have babies.'

'I found it. Why illegal?'

'Everything is illegal,' he whispered, parting the curtains cautiously to peer out. 'Damn near.' The face upon Glen's big, pink, cubical head looked somewhat drawn.

'What's the matter?'

'Oh, nothing,' he said testily. 'We're going to have a gas war, that's all.'

Glen was a pathetic figure as he moved so as not to cast a shadow on the curtains. His bright, skin-tight plastic suit was far from skin-tight, and even his cape looked baggy.

'Is it? Is that all?'

'No. Say, that neighbor of ours has been raking leaves an awfully long time.'

'Answer me. What's wrong? Something at the office?'

'Everything. The carbon paper and stamps and paper clips have begun to disappear. I'm afraid they'll blame me. The boss is going to buy a computer to keep track of the loss. Someone stole my ration book on the train, and I found I had last week's newspaper. IBM stock is falling, faintly falling. I have a cold, or something. And – and they're doing away with the Dewey Decimal System.'

'You're just overwrought. Why don't you just sit down and dandle our new baby on your knee, while I rustle up some supper.'

'Stealing food! It's indecent!'

'Everyone does it, dear. Did you know I found the baby in the oven?'

'No!'

'Yes, the queerest thing. I had just been wishing for a baby, and there it was.'

'How are the other appliances doing?'

'The automatic washer tried to devour me. The dishwater is fading away; we must have missed a payment.'

'Yes, and we're overdrawn,' he said, sighing.

'The garbage disposal is hulking.'

'Hulking?'

'Over there.'

He did not look where she was pointing. He continued to peer out the window, where the weather situation was building up. A Welcome Wagon moved slowly down the street. He could not read the sign, but he recognized the armor plating and the blue snouts of machine-guns.

'Yes, it just sits there hulking in the sink, and it won't eat anything. It ate its guarantee, though.'

The neighbor, a 'Mr Green', paused in his raking to note down the Welcome Wagon's license number.

'Not hulking, darling. *Sulking*,' Glen said.

'You have such a big vocabulary. And you don't even read "How to Build Big Words".'

'I read *Existential Digest*, when I find the time,' he confessed. 'But last week I took their test and learned that I'm not alienated enough. That's why I'm so damned proud of our kids.'

'Jenny and Peter?'

'The same.'

Agnes sighed. 'I'd like to read a copy of the *Irish Mail* some time. By the way, the potatoes had poison again. Every eye.' She went into the bedroom and laid the baby in its crib.

'I'm going down and turn something on the lathe,' Glen announced. 'Something good.'

'Take off your cape first. You remember the safety laws we learned at PTA.'

'Lord, how could I forget? Snuff out all candles. Never stand in a canoe or bathtub. Give name, rank and serial number only. Accept checks only if endorsed in your presence. Do not allow rats to chew on matches, should they so desire.'

He disappeared, and at the same time, Jenny and Peter came home from school, demanding a 'snack'. Agnes gave them Hungarian goulash, bread and butter, coffee and apple pie. They paid 95 cents each, and each tipped her 15 cents. They were gruff, dour eight-year-olds who talked little while they ate. Agnes was a little afraid of them. After their snack, they belted on guns and went out to hunt other children, before it grew too dark to see them.

Agnes sighed and sat down to her secret transmitter.

'AUNT ROSE EXPECTED BY NOON TRAIN,' she sent. 'HAVE MADE ARRGTS FOR HER GLADIOLI. SEE THAT FUDGE MEETS 0400 PARIS PLANE WITH CANDLES. THE GARDNER NEEDS TROWEL XPRESS.'

In a moment, the reply came. 'TROWEL ARRGD. FUDGE HAS NO REPEAT NO CANDLES. WILL USE DDT. HOLD ROSE TILL VIOLET HEARD FROM.'

Always the same, tired, meaningless messages. Agnes hid her transmitter in the cookie jar as Glen came up the stairs. He had his own transmitter in the basement, she was sure of that. For all she could tell, it was him she was calling each evening.

'Look at this!' he said proudly, and displayed a newel post.

Outside, a plane dropped leaflets. The neighbor rushed about, raking them up and burning them.

'Every night, the same damned thing,' said Glen, grinding his teeth. 'Every night they drop leaflets telling us to give up, and every night that bastard burns them all. At this rate, we'll never even learn who "they" are.'

'Is it really so important?' she asked. He would not answer. 'Come on, quit hulking. I'll tell you what I want to do. I want to ride on a realway train.'

'*Rail*way,' he corrected. 'You can't, the Public Health Department says that going more than thirty miles an hour contributes significantly to cancer.'

'A lot you care what happens to me!'

Glen bowed his great cube of a head resignedly over the television set. 'You'll notice,' he said, 'that it looks like an innocent Army–Navy football game. And so it may be. Perhaps the ball won't blow up when he kicks it. Perhaps that series of plays is only a coincidence.'

'Number twenty-seven fades back to pass,' she murmured. 'What would that mean, I wonder?'

Glen felt her hand reach out to touch his. He held hands with his wife in the darkened living-room, after making sure she was not wearing her poison ring.

'The common cold,' he muttered. '*They* call it the "common cold". By the way, have I told you we're overdrawn?'

'Yes. It's that damned car. You would have to order all those special features.'

'The bazooka in the trunk? The direction-finder radio? The gun turret? Everyone else had had them for years, Agnes. What am I supposed to do if the police start chasing me? Try to outrun them, me with all that armor plate weighing me down?'

'I just don't see what we're going to live on,' she said.

'We can eat green stamps until—'

'No, they confiscated them this morning. I forgot to tell you.'

The children trooped in, smelling of mud and cordite. Jenny had scratched her knee on a barbed-wire barrier. Agnes applied a bandaid to it, and gave them coffee and doughnuts, 15 cents. Then she sent them upstairs to brush their teeth.

'And don't, for God's sake, use the tap water,' Glen shouted. 'There's something in it.' He walked into the room where the baby slept and returned in a minute, shaking his head. 'Could have sworn I heard him ticking.'

'Oh, Glen, let's get away for a few days. Let's go to the country.'

'Oh sure. Travel twenty miles over mined roads to look at a couple of cowpies. You wouldn't dare get out of the car, for fear of the deadly snakes. And they've sowed the ground with poison ivy and giant viruses.'

'I wouldn't care! Just a breath of fresh air—'

'Sure. Nerve gas. Mustard gas. Tear gas. *Pollen.* Even if we survived, we'd be arrested. No one ever goes into the country any more but dope peddlers, looking for wild tobacco.'

Agnes began to cry. Everyone was someone else. No one was who they were. The garbageman scrutinized her messages to the milkman. In the park, the pigeons all wore metal capsules taped to their legs. There were cowpies in the country, but no cows. Even at the supermarket you had to be careful. If you picked out items that seemed to form any sort of pattern...

'Are there any popsicles left?' Glen asked.

'No. There's nothing in the icebox but some leftover custard. We can't eat that, it has a map in it. Glen, what *are* we going to eat?'

'I don't know. How about . . . the baby? Well, don't look at me like that! You found him in the oven, didn't you? Suppose you'd just lit the oven without looking inside?'

'No! I will not give up my baby for a – casserole!'

'All right, all right! I was merely making a suggestion, that's all.'

It was dark now, throughout the lead-walled house, except in the kitchen. Out the quartz picture window, dusk was falling on the lawn, on the lifeless body of 'Mr Green'. The television showed a panel discussion of eminent doctors, who wondered if eating were not the major cause of insanity.

Agnes went to answer the front door, while Glen went back to the kitchen.

'Excuse me,' the priest said to Agnes. 'I'm on a sick call. Someone was good enough to loan me his Diaper Service truck, but I'm afraid it has broken down. I wonder if I might use your phone?'

'Certainly, Father. It's bugged, of course.'

'Of course.'

She stood aside to let him pass, and just then Glen shouted, 'The baby! He's at the custard!'

Agnes and the priest dashed out to see. In the clean, well-lighted kitchen, Glen stood gaping at the open refrigerator. Somehow the baby had got it open, for now Agnes could see his diapered bottom and pink toes sticking out from a lower shelf.

'He's hungry,' she said.

'Take another look,' grated Glen.

Leaning closer she saw the child had pulled the map from the custard. He was taking photos of it with a tiny, baby-sized camera.

'Microfilm!' she gasped.

'Who are you?' Glen asked the priest.

'I'm—'

'Wait a minute. You don't look like a man of the cloth to me.'

It was true, Agnes saw in the light. The breeze rustled the carbon-paper cassock, and she saw it was held together with paper clips. His stole was, on closer examination, a strip of purple stamps.

'If you're a priest,' Glen continued, 'why do I see on your Roman collar *the letterhead of my office*?'

'Very clever of you,' said the man, drawing a pistol from his sleeve. 'I'm sorry you saw through our little ruse. Sorry for you, that is.'

'*Our?*' Glen looked at the baby. 'Hold on. Agnes, what kind of a vehicle did he drive up in?'

'A diaper truck.'

'Aha! I've been waiting a long time to catch up with you – Diaper Man. Your chequered career has gone on far too long.'

'Ah, so you've recognized me and my dimple-kneed assistant, have you? But I'm afraid it won't do you much good. You see, we already have the photos, and there is a bullet here for each of you. Don't try to stop us!'

Watching them, the false priest scooped up the baby. 'I think I had better kill the two of you in any case,' he said. 'You already know too much about my *modus operandi.*' The baby in his arms waved the camera gleefully and gooed its derision.

'All right,' said Diaper Man. 'Face the wall, please.'

'Now!' said Glen. He leaped for the gun, while Agnes deftly kicked the camera from the baby's chubby fist.

The infant spy looked startled, but he acted fast, a tiny blur of motion. Scooping up two fistfuls of custard, he flung them in Glen's eyes. Gasping, Glen dropped the gun, as the infamous pair made their dash for freedom.

'You'll never take me alive!' snarled the false priest, vaulting into his truck.

'Let them go,' said Glen. He tasted the custard. 'I should have realized earlier the baby wasn't ticking, he was *clicking.* But let them go; they won't get far anyway, and we've saved the map. For whatever it's worth.'

'Are you all right, darling?'

'Fine. Mmmm. This is pretty good, Agnes.'

She blushed at the compliment. There was a muffled explosion, and in the distance they could see flames shooting high in the air.

'Esso bombing the Shell station,' said Glen. The gas war had begun.

Undecember

Besides being the 11th (or 13th) month, Undecember is meant to correct the more serious errors of our calendar:

THE CYCLIC ERROR. We expect every Saturday to be followed by a Sunday, every twelve by a one o'clock, and every December by a January. Yet our only evidence for these cycles comes from the clocks and calendars we have ourselves made to mark these cycles.

This circular reasoning began before the second century of our era, when Marcus Manilius wrote:

'Thrones have perished, peoples passed from domination to slavery, from captivity to empire, but the same months of the year have always brought up on the horizon the same stars.'

This assertion contains the seeds of its own refutation: A slave cannot see the same stars as a free man, while a dead man (Manilius is now dead) cannot see stars at all. Without continual observations made by men who remain alive over the eons, we cannot be sure that the bright points of light in the sky are what Manilius called 'stars'.

Others have carried the cyclic error to its two possible extremes: In A.D. 628, Brahmagupta declared that the world is destroyed by fire and recreated once every 4,320,000,000 years. On the other hand, Buddhist writers have seen a different cycle, in which the world is destroyed and created anew 75,000 times each second. But we fall into the same abyss in saying that Winter has returned, or that it's March again.

THE RIVER ERROR. The numbering of days in each month, or of years, supposes that time flows on in an orderly progression, like a series of numbers. Mr L. Sterne, among others, has proved that it does not.

THE TORTOISE ERROR. This, the most serious fault in our calendar system, assumes that time moves at all. It is self-evident that time is as motionless as the tortoise.

The simplest solution is not to abandon our calendar, but to introduce an unexpected month: Undecember. It may be shuffled in among other calendar pages, to break the predictable pattern of flow. Or it may be ignored entirely; the very knowledge of its existence is enough to demonstrate that time has no revolution, no progression, no movement and in fact no qualities whatever.

Undecember records days wasted in waiting, spent in dreaming, gathered up in trivial memories.

It records days which somehow get away from us, or come upon us without warning.

It records days looked forward to, which never arrive; days we wish were over or wish would never end; days we must recall but cannot; and days of which we can say nothing.

It records the *déjà vu* moment; the entire life of the amnesiac; the tomorrows of the improvident; and all the anniversaries of time.

Sun	Mon	Tue	Wed	Thu	Fri	Sat
	17	11	16	8	23	3
14	22	7	19	24	15	8
26	8	20	21	14	20	6
22	6	25	28	11	4	27
11	0	25				

Some Notable Anniversaries:

17TH: Anniversary of Heraclitus' river-error: 'One cannot go down to the river twice.' We still speak of time as a river, flowing out of the tributaries of the future, down through the present, and on down to the delta of the past, where it deposits all the shit and silt we call History. But there's something wrong with this image: All that flows flows at some speed. Time, then, must also flow at some speed (measured in hours per hour) which we could find out. Using some meta-clock, or time-speedometer, we could then time time, to decide whether an hour really passes as slowly as it seems.

What's wrong with it all, is that time would then be measured against some other time which could itself flow . . . and could in turn be measured . . . so on to an infinite series. This seems unfair.

11TH: Next Sunday, a Tuesday a few weeks ago, or today (Thursday). There is no contradiction in holding all three times in one's mind at the same time. Perhaps all are the anniversary of some impending, long-forgotten event.

16TH: Unbirthday of Charles Lutwidge Dodgson, who invented the unbirthday. He was born on January 27th and died 13 days earlier.

8TH: *Bank Computer Holiday*, England and Wales. Computers, operating in what is called 'real time', are considered real entities.

8TH: Might also be written the 1/8th of the month. Notice that days in this month are not numbered serially, because any series 1,2,3, . . . implies a future and a past which may or may not exist. In the same way, our method of numbering the years promises that a year '1984' will arrive, and that a year '1884' has passed. For this reason, Undecember is numbered randomly.

23RD: On January 22nd, 1932, the USSR began its second Five-Year Plan, again demonstrating the fallibility of number as a means of measuring and controlling time.

3RD: In 1899, Alfred Jarry wrote 'How to Construct a Time Machine'. He died in 1907. In 1913, as Marcel Proust, he began scribbling about time once again. This has led some to suppose that Jarry somehow succeeded in building his time machine. A simple disproof of this follows:

Had Jarry succeeded, he might have travelled back in time and assisted at the difficult breech-birth of his own grandfather. He might indeed have been the clumsy male midwife who caused the infant's death – a man using the alias 'Marcel Proust' but who is otherwise unknown. But others have shown that the midwife was not Alfred Jarry; moreover the real Proust had no access to the time machine built by H. G. Wells to Jarry's instructions. QED, 'How to Construct a Time Machine' is fiction, developed without the assistance of a midwiving author.

14TH: Pendulum clock invented by Christiaan Huygens, 1656.

22ND: On January 22nd, 1932, the USSR began its second Five-Year Plan, again demonstrating the infallibility of number as a means of measuring and controlling time.

7TH: Another river-day: On June 7th, 1849, between 4.10 and 4.11 a.m., we are told*, Huckleberry Finn awakens on his river-raft. He perceives 'stars', and 'then he sinks into an immemorial sleep that envelops him like murky water'; real worlds and their times are no more than an interruption in the dream of a fictional character, himself not entirely believable, but dreamed up by someone using the name 'Mark Twain' (river slang again), whose real name, we are told, was Samuel Clemens. Clemens, of course, does not exist. There is a chance that he once existed, if only in the fertile delta of the imagination of Jorge Luis Borges.

19TH: Non-discovery of two celestial objects, OH 471 and 4C 05.34, said to be the oldest objects in the universe, being primeval galaxies. Radiation from these objects has taken the

* See Borges, 'A New Refutation of Time' where 'Borges' appears to doubt his own reality.

entire lifetime of the universe to reach the University of Texas at Austin.

24TH: Persons using a special device at the Institute for Parapsychology, Durham, North Carolina, have shown an uncanny ability to see into the future, 1/250,000th of a second.

15TH: It was not on the 15th Undecember 1938 that paleontologist Marjorie Courtenay-Latimer discovered among the catch of a South African trawler a fish called the coelacanth, previously thought to have been extinct for several million years.

8TH: Anniversary of a week ago Thursday.

26TH: J. W. Dunne, in *An Experiment with Time*, shows how dreams not only come true, but everything else works, too.

8TH: At noon, GMT, on December 8th, 1859, Admiral Henry Fitt set out on his famous round-the-world 'Beat the Sun' cruise. Sail, oar and special elastic engines enabled him to keep a constant westerly speed of 460 knots, staying ahead of the Sun. In principle this meant that, when he had circumnavigated the globe, shipboard time would be (still) noon of the 14th, while shore time would be noon of the 15th. He intended to recoup the enormous cost of the cruise by reading advance copies of the newspaper stock market reports, and gaining a 24-hour jump on other investors. This scheme seems to have failed in some way, and the controversy it aroused led to the establishment of the International Dateline, which ships are forbidden to cross for 24 hours at a time.

20TH: St Zeno's Day. Zeno proved motion to be impossible, since even the slightest motion must require an eternity of time to be completed. The proof of this has never been completed.

21ST: The discovery of *entropy* proves time to be neither a river nor a turning wheel, but merely a direction. Entropy means disorder, and as we move forward in time, disorder increases. Thus when we watch a film, we know whether it is running forward or backward by entropic indications: A pane of glass is shattered, a banana peeled and eaten, a tortoise drops on the head of Aeschylus and kills him – all indicating forward movement in time. A shattered pane coming together, a banana disgorged and reclothed in its skin, or Aeschylus coming to life, standing up and firing a tortoise off his head into the air – negative entropy, or backward movement in time. Time is an arrow.

14TH: Black Saturday. Henry Ford says: 'History is bunk', but proves automotion possible.

20TH: St Zeno's Day. Zeno said that, for an arrow to reach its target, it must first move $\frac{1}{2}$ the distance, then $\frac{1}{2}$ of the remaining distance, and so on: $\frac{1}{2} + \frac{1}{4} + 1/8 + \ldots$, an infinite series that can never be completed in a finite time. Likewise he arranged a race between Achilles and a tortoise (or perhaps Aeschylus and a tortoise) proving that same point. Time to Zeno must have seemed an arrow divisible into an infinite number of points. He did not believe the story of Aeschylus' death – how an eagle dropped a tortoise on his head – even though such a death seemed to fulfil an oracle. The oracle said that Aeschylus would die from a blow from heaven. Rational Zeno would have said it meant no more than an instant bolt of lightning.

6TH: Discovery of the speed of light, 186,000 miles per second.

22ND: Believing in history is like believing oracles. The past is a phantom like the future. Nevertheless, the USSR put great trust in both: Having awakened on their river raft from one dream of a Five-Year Plan, they dozed and dreamt of a second to come.

6TH: The speed of light being known, Einstein was able to dazzle the world with his special theory of relativity. It declares that, to an observer moving at the speed of light, there is no time. An arrow and a tortoise fired at one another at the speed of light, to us will seem to collide instantly. Nevertheless, the tortoise will himself have an eternity in which to contemplate his impending death. To him, the arrow will be Zeno's arrow, suspended forever at a safe distance.

25TH: A suitable founding date for the fictitious United States of America, home of Huckleberry Finn again, awake. In honour of Undecembrist philosophers and poets, the United States took its emblem and slogan from Zeno. That many points in time cluster together to form a continuum, they express as *One from Many* (E Pluribus Unum), below an eagle, holding arrows and bolts of lightning. On its breast are 'stars'.

28TH: Reputed founding of *Time* magazine by Henry Luce (= 'light').

4TH: The Babylonian New Years Day (1st of Nisan) began on April 4th, 786 B.C.

27TH: In the Bodleian Library there recently existed an uncatalogued item, namely an almanack, containing entries of a peculiar nature. Under 'Gardening tips' it recommended ways of glueing petals on to blossoms ('You'll be rewarded by the sight of these blossoms closing into beautiful little buds'); glueing dead branches on to the cut stumps of tree-limbs; planting whole carrots and later digging up carrot seed; depollination, etc.

Under 'Astrology' it described persons having a letter full of important news, which they then sealed up and gave to the postman to deliver to the sender; it spoke of useful advice from a friend, which was first followed and then received; it spoke of many famous persons who had died in Taurus, but subsequently lived long and useful lives.

Of world events, it spoke of a peace treaty between two major nations, from which the signature had recently been removed; war would follow. The main concern in wartime, evidently, was for the millions of new lives which would be created – to cope with such a population boom would require, eventually, an enormous number of pregnancies. Again, could the farmers cope with the great volume of food which these new millions would expel? The land seems hardly able to bear the burden of such bumper crops as will appear, nor are the farmers, in the foreseeable past, able to pay for such crops.

The entire book went on in this way, even to its advertisements, for wrecked cars, worn-out shoes, fingernail parings and other body wastes. For adolescent readers, a certain cream guarantees the eruption of real pimples, as no other cream or lotion can do. Broken appliances are said to add filth to clothing 'scientifically' (when they begin working), to remove heat from cooked foods, to stain teeth or scuff shoes to a low shine. Electronic apparatus promises to remove radio or stereo noises from any room.

This almanack no longer exists. Having reached its own copyright date, it was of course sent to the printers to have ink removed from its pages, to be pulped and processed, and now it is a coniferous tree in Finland, where they say it loses one ring per year, disappearing up its own annulation, annually. There is some question as to what becomes of it: It may be that, reaching the seed or cone, it will then grow up again in some negative time, becoming once more a solid tree and finally cut down to make matches, one of which will strike a light at some necessary moment. (Proust begins his story by striking a match to look at his watch. Nearly midnight.)

0TH: C. L. Dodgson, another unbirthday. Author of 'What the Tortoise Said to Achilles' (*Mind*, December 1894). What the tortoise does say would take an infinite number of pages to record, though this difficulty might be overcome by removing the ink from earlier pages and re-using them, in an endless cycle . . .

25TH: Dodgson lies awake at night compounding his 'Pillow Problems', vain exercises in infinity to help pass the invalid hours. Proust has been watching the streak of light beneath his bedroom door, unable to decide whether it is midnight gaslight or dawn. Zeno turns in restless sleep, in his nightmare running slowly, dragging old tortoise feet through mud to escape the arrow that comes ever infinitesimally closer without striking. Huckleberry Finn lands on the shores of sleep safely, after his moment of drifting awake, seeing unfamiliar points of light; he may remember a single star, but the wrong one: It exploded into nothing 4,320,000,000 years before the Earth was born, and nothing remains but its false light. Aeschylus at breakfast tells his wife his dream: 'It was raining tortoises and . . .' And Manilius squats watching the horizon at dawn in an act of faith.

The Great Wall of Mexico

1. Washington Crossing the Yangtze

His predecessor had kept tape recorders running in every room, catching his 'thoughts' as he paced. But then his predecessor, Rogers, had always been a flamboyant action-man leader, the first Secret Service agent to be elevated to the position he guarded with his profile. His career spanned a few headlines:

GBM SAVED FROM SHOOTING
HERO BODYGUARD TO RUN FOR SENATE
SEN. ROGERS WILL RUN
ROGERS WINS!
ROGERS ASSASSINATED

Before the assassin could confess, the police station at which he was held blew up, along with a fair piece of Mason City surrounding it. The FBI found the cause to be a gas leak of an unusual type. On succeeding to the office of Great Seal, our man promoted the investigating agent, K. Homer Bissell, to bureau chief.

Our man kept his thoughts on specially printed forms:

Presidential Notes PN/1/1776
President ....
Date:......................., 199........

General Subject:	Committee/ Commission/ Cabinet Referral:	Presidential Remarks:
....	....	....
....	....	....
....	....	....

There were also memoranda, agenda, briefs and résumés always stacked on top of the elegant polished* desk. The Great Seal liked to be well supplied with business at hand. It enabled him to expedite and finalize things with obvious efficiency at any time, ready to deal with work and get it out of the way before he relaxed, working hard to play even harder, making his guiding principle Throughput.

MEMO: From the President

I do not tolerate noisy press conferences. If possible, the next press conference should be arranged to maximize silence.

I, the state, further do not like science fiction cops. If it is really necessary for them to wear those helmets, plastic visors, tunics, gauntlets and jump boots, will they please keep out of my sight.

'I can see how this is going to build up into something,' Filcup warns. 'Remember when he didn't like certain news analysts? My God, remember when he didn't like brown eggs?'

Karl Wax brought up the subject of uniforms at the Tuesday meeting of Special Advisers. His 'birthday cake' suggestion was voted down ('We have to make a pleasing offering to the President, but this is ridiculous. Anyway, a naked guard is just the kind of thing that could backfire. We all know how He feels about nakedness') and Dan Foyle gained the upper hand with 'a uniform of evening clothes, slightly modified in some distinctive manner – anyone who's seen Turhan Bey and Susanna Foster in *The Climax* will know what I mean. This has been a long and bloody war – though not pointless or without compensations – and He sorely needs a little formal relaxation.'

Agenda for Wednesday

Commission stamps to commemorate Walt Disney, Louisa May Alcott, Ty Cobb; provisionally Billy Mitchell, Ralph Nader. Check figs on Indochina: Gen. H. claims 2,250 megatons reqd for reconditioning, Op. Orpheus. Check position on Tanzania

* And bulletproof, another legacy of poor Rogers.

vis-à-vis South African bloc. Could recredit our reputation in Brazil, renew Arab franchise.

Presentation of award from Mothers of American Insurrection (blue suit). Read speech of Q's for decontamination efforts, constitutional loopholes. Lunch with leading blacks. Press conference on Martha's blood clot. *Important*: p.m. conference with Bissell, psychologists, police reps on physical/mental reconciliation of disaffiliatees, dealing with *radical element.*

While Tichner and Groeb arrange his urgent memos, he runs over the morning mail résumé, made up as a composite letter:

Dear Mr President:

While 47% of me would like to congratulate you on your courageous stand on the Chile question, 21% of me also wonders if you've lived up to our expectations regarding . . . and though 17% of me disagrees, a massive 36% thinks you handled the Moral Pollution bill wisely, and for the rest, I can't make up my mind.

Sincere good wishes,
Your friend,
J. Q. Public

Suggested Uniforms for White House Police
Brocade, knee breeks and periwigs
Minutemen, 'dressed for Sunday'
Student Prince
Uncle Sam
Henry Clay gaiters, panamas
Christy's Minstrels
Custer's cavalry
Commodore Perry
Rough Riders
The Climax
Mysterious Island
Dickensian ragamuffins (struck off, replaced by 'Leopard tuxes and light-up bow ties')
Texas A & M

Diamond Horseshoe
Each Night I Die
Zoot blues
Nice neat business

The GS follows no suggestions, however. For a time, while he reads a digested condensation of the life of FDR, the palace guards are persuaded to imitate that eminence. Bang seven-thirty every morning the guardroom doors slide back and out rolls a parade of large-jawed men in gleaming wheelchairs, champing their cigarette holders and assuring the President that he has nothing to fear but fear itself. And even that phase is preferable, they all agree, to his Peter Stuyvesant period.

After the mail, his condensed news digest:

Wednesday, February 12th
PRESIDENT SIGNS CONTROVERSIAL DUCK BILL. Conservation leaders praise forward-thinking leader. President disclaims, says only small step forward, but 'little strokes fell great oaks'.
President To Announce New Peace Plan
President's Wife Feared Ill
Cabinet Changes?

He was vaguely aware that the real press hardly ever mentioned him; these items had been gleaned from the *Rood City Post*, the *Oslo* (Nevada) *Times* and the *Budget Junction O'erseer*. He knew the press laughed at him for his sincerity, for his supposed vanity, for the way he conducted the war. They crucified him if he looked solemn, and when he smiled there were unkind remarks about his woodenness. The press! What did they know? Let them go on calling him an unsaleable commodity, a snap, an empty suit. They would one day look the ape!

Not a Gem
During morning coffee, he felt like a visit to the Reagan Room, but curbed it (PRESIDENT MASTERS OWN CONDITION). There

was still the award ceremony (The confounded press! More pix with eyes closed, mouth open) and the luncheon with its precarious handshakes. And first of all there was Operation Orpheus and fat, freckled General Hare.

'We call it Orpheus, sir, because there's no turning back. We thought of calling it Operation Lot, but people might get it confused with Operation Sandlot, our talent-recruiting program, and with Operation Big Sandy. Operation Sodom was even worse. So we—'

'Get to the point, Hare. Where do you get this figure of 2,250 megatons?'

The general set down his coffee cup carelessly, so that the cookie fell from its saucer perch. Disorder. Reagan Room. Operation. Or Free Us. The music of the nukebox means a dance with China. I'd like to get you. On a slow boat. China, angina, regina, vagina.

'Let's see now.' General Hare jotted figures on the edge of a soggy paper napkin. 'We have North Zone, South Zone, Countries Able, Baker, Charlie, Dog . . .'

Slow bull to china.

'That makes 1,939,424 square kilometers, and that comes out to only 749 megatons. Allowing a 300 percent margin for error, we get 2,250 megatons, say 150 warheads. We wouldn't hardly miss it.'

'Haha! Oh, excuse me, general, I just thought of something. What kind of – ha – boat would a slow boat to China be? Eh? Eh?'

'I don't exactly get you, sir. You mean—?'

'It's a riddle, man! Just tell me the answer to that, and I may give you the green light on one of these operations.'

'Mr President! I—'

'Give up? Give up?'

There was some argument about whether the general had actually given up before the President told him the answer. To placate him, it finally became necessary to okay Operation Big Sandy, both phases.

A Lexicon of Governmental Report Terms
alienatee: person not sympathetic to the government
bugs: demonstrators (hence swatting a swarm: riot control)
dealienation: brainwashing
decontamination: shock therapy used in dealienation
disaffiliate: anarchist
maverick: businessman who defects to radical side
opinion analyst: police agent
rationalizing an increment: stopping a demonstration
reconciliation: interrogation with extreme force
rodeo: suspect roundup and intensive reconciliation
social therapist: interrogator
technicality: prisoner.

Souplines
The President has a rich dream life. It soaks through his skin like a rich soup and arranges the wrinkles in his 'sober' business suit. Examination of the seat of the President's business pants reveals inmost desires, claims psychologist. A relief map of Indochina, perhaps.

His dreams boil up in projects, plans, operations, advisory committee schemes. His dreaming eye is on the donut, says aide. Operation Big Sandy, for instance. It may seem crazy to wall off Mexico (phase one), but there you are. 'It's so crazy,' says General Hare, 'it *just might work*. Or not.'

The lunch with leading blacks goes even worse than he'd feared. The press conference is canceled and he disappears for half an hour into the Reagan Room. Later, before he goes to meet concerned psychologists and policemen, he checks his chin for lines of sin.

Major Operation
Operation Big Sandy was born on the littered conference table of the Great Seal's team of 'creative' advisers. Karl and Dan were cutting and folding maps to rearrange the world. Filcup sought truth in the depths of black coffee.

'A door-to-door instant welfare program? Let me call it Streetheart.'

'A national idea bank—'

'Yes, but unemployment.'

'Unemployment, sure, but social security deficits.'

Filcup held up an atlas. 'Think of the United States as a sheep or cow, marked into cuts of meat.'

'The United Steaks?'

'Don't laugh, it's the body politic. About to be invaded by hostile germs, coming up the anus from Mexico—'

'Now just hold on a minute!' Texas Dan Foyle demanded that Filcup apologize.

'What we need is antiseptic. Make the Rio Grande radioactive. Build a wall,' he continued.

'A wall to write on!' Karl said. 'A challenge for our painters.'

'Sell off advertising space.'

Dan cracked his knuckles with unrestrained excitement. 'This could be great for the old folks. Give them something to look at, a new interest in life. You realize that there are over a hundred retirement ranches in that area, and that more than half our retired folks live within a hundred miles of Mexico.'

Filcup seemed convulsed by a private joke. 'Wait till I tell you the rest, Dan. There's something in this for the old folks, all right, in phase two. But for now, we'll not only sell space to advertisers, we'll build gas stations, highways, concessions. A view of the wall. A view over it. Visit the gun emplacements. Amazing plastic replicas of the Grand Canyon, the Great Wall of China, the Wailing Wall of Jerusalem! It'll take up the slack in Mexican tourism, giving our vacationers a new place to go. And of course it'll be a sop for unemployment.'

'The Great Wall!' They toasted it in cold coffee.

2. Technicalities

At Fort Nixon Retraining Center

Dr Veck was explaining the routine to the new man, Lane. 'I know youngsters like you are chock-full of theory, itching to try everything out,' he said, clapping him on the shoulder. 'Fort Nixon is just the place for it. The normal routine isn't too irksome because most of ours are politicals, as you know. Not much trouble except security – they will try to escape – but I'm afraid they make dull cases.'

He slid open a panel depicting the death of Actaeon (or some other deer) to show, through the back of a one-way glass, a dozen retrainees at work on handicrafts. 'As you see, dull.'

'Oh, I don't know. Who's the old-timer over in the corner? The one doing leather work.'

'Old Hank? He's pretty well beyond treatment. I'll show you his record sometime. Looks as if he's making another bridle. He's made three already, one white, one red and one black. This one seems to be beige. Of course he has no idea what he'll do with them. In fact, he told me he knows nothing at all about horses. Poor old Hank!'

Oblivious to their concern, Hank was kicking a water pipe under his bench, tapping out a message to his one friend.

'The government apparently has contingency plans to use some of our people for a work camp. Some construction project. I'd guess it's either another retirement ranch or else a dam on the Rio Grande. But of course they never tell us anything. We only have to deal with the extra security that will mean.'

'Do you have many escapes?' asked Dr Lane.

'We always catch them. And then we give them a taste of the random room. Little invention of my own. The occupant doesn't know what will happen to him, or when – all he knows is that it will be unpleasant. At perfectly random intervals he gets cold water, hot water, shock, strobe lights, whistles, drones, a shower of shit, whispers, heat, cold and so on. Life in the ordinary ward seems pretty good to them after that. They're grateful for a secure, comfortable routine, and escape is – well – remote.'

'Ah, yes, I noticed your paper on it in *Political Psychopath*, though I didn't have a chance to read it yet. Sounds interesting.'

Dr Veck acknowledged this half compliment with half a

smile. 'Your praxis was at Mount Burris, was it not?' He found his hair hurt, and his breath had to be forced.

'Yes, but not with politicals. I worked mainly with the children of malcontents. Primary adjustments, corporation workshop. Tame stuff compared to political deviation, which has always been my first love. Are you all right, doctor?'

'Ah, it's nothing. I experience these symptoms, shortness of breath and so on, whenever I leave my office for any length of time. What say we go up to my office now, and I'll show you some typical case histories.'

Entering Veck's office, the two men were arrested by a throbbing desert sunset. Dr Lane sighed. Breaking off in the middle of a discussion of pattern attrition, he murmured:

> 'Who captains haughty Nature in her flaming hair
> Can ne'er rest slothy whilst some lesser groom—'

'What was that?' Veck snapped the blinds shut and turned up the decent office light.

'Nothing, really. I wrote it for a class in Environmental Humanities.'

'Good for you! We social engineers can use a smattering of culture around the place. Gives us new perspective on our problems. Like this one, for instance.' He threw a dusty folder on the desk. 'Mr C. was a Communist, and he liked being a Communist. We tried damned near everything. Finally we learned that a fellow party member had seduced C.'s wife. We simply told him about this, allowed him to escape, and bingo!'

'Bingo?'

'By killing the seducer, C. proved that he thought of his wife as a piece of property. It was the first beachhead of capitalism in his commie brain. With our help he became vitally interested in other possessions, in getting and spending. His socialism fell away like an old scab. Today C. is a Baptist minister and a Rotarian.'

'Amazing!'

'Or take this case, Mr von J. Von J. was a malcontent, a hater of authority. Arrested for vandalism, jaywalking, nonpayment of taxes, contempt of court. Here we used aversive methods to great effect. The first step was to teach him *self-discipline*. We made him hold his urine twenty hours at a time, memorize chapters of Norman Vincent Peale, and so on. Now, I am given to understand, von J. is more than a model citizen; he does some work for the FBI.

'Mr B. was an anarchist. We placed him in a controlled work situation. Among those who worked around him we removed everyone of competence and replaced them with indecisive idiots. They looked to B. for guidance; he became a straw boss, then a real boss. We rewarded his responsibility with more pay and privileges. He became a trusty.

'Naturally he escaped. On his return, B. learned that R., one of the idiot workers who had worshiped him, had, left on his own, committed suicide.

'In this way B. was brought to see that running away doesn't bring liberty, but slavery. He now realized that the truly free aren't rebels and anarchists, but those who have submitted their will to a Higher Authority. The way I put it to him in a little talk was: "Democracy is like a spaceship. It may seem stuffy inside, but you can't just step out for a breath of outer space!" '

Dr Lane saw his cue, and chuckled. 'But how did you really arrange it? What actually happened to R.? A transfer?'

'Oh, dear me, no.' Veck laughed. 'We had to string him up in his room, for real. To make it look good. B. was nothing if not skeptical.'

Remorse Code Message

O Hank! You have turnt your face to the wall again. Or anyway you've stopped acknowledging my messages. And you won't talk to the other retrainees. Sit there then in the common room, silent and obscure as Gun.* Trying perhaps to etch out a certain territory in the room by exposing it to the acid of your silence. One by one the others move away to far parts of the room where they can kibbitz at Ping-Pong or pretend to study the paper autumn leaves pinned to the bulletin board, wishing

* War god of the Fon.

all a HAPPY COLUMBUS DAY. Perhaps you can empty the room itself, even the wing, or the whole of Fort Nixon, driving away all life and plastering over the crevices with thick hostile silence.

But you just couldn't have such an unconstructive notion. Not to say such an asocial, dangerous notion. Because whatever they say about there being no punishments here, extremely uncomfortable things can happen to the asocial. And your silence can hardly be construed as 'making an honest effort' at retraining, can it?

Your obstinate silence. Suppose they feel it necessary to counter it? To bring in the Fort Nixon Silver Band to fill the void? And then certain select retrainees (the 'doctors' staying out of it) might hold you to a chair while the Silver Band marches past, playing 'Under the Double Eagle' and 'Them Basses'. Certain select retrainees, known somehow to one another, might hold you to a chair while the Silver Band sharpens up. They sharpen the edges of the bells of their trumpets and sousaphones. Then they extend your tongue and hold it while they saw it off with their shining instruments. Then they pin it to the bulletin board, among the autumn leaves.

Listen, Hank, you have friends in high places. One phone call and you can be out of here, long gone before they put you to work on the Great Project. Just admit that God is pretty first-rate and God's Own Country is, gosh, not so bad either, when you get right down under it. Or say anything, say howdy to your friends and neighbors, the other inmates. Otherwise I hear the Silver Band massing in the anteroom; I see a wet pink leaf upon the bulletin board, HAPPY COLUMBUTH DAY, end of Message.

Dr Lane's Secret Journal (I)

. . . the question of who he thinks he is trying to contact. Veck claims he was in prison before, tapped out morse code on the water pipes with other prisoners and just couldn't break the habit. Though no one here seems to listen to his tapping.

Yesterday, I tried immobilizing Hank with s.p. and restraints. As I predicted, he keeps messages going even then, by nearly inaudible tongue clicks.

A challenging case. Hank evidently was some kind of painter and sculptor at one time. Later he made a series of animated cartoons of which I saw only one example. It seemed particularly sadistic to me. The main story seemed to be a quarrel between dogs, cats and mice. This version differed from others mainly in that it strove for realistic violence. Thus when an animal was struck by an enormous wooden mallet, he did not go dizzy with X X eyes and tweeting birds and a pulsating red lump. Instead he screamed, staggered, fell, gushed blood, vomited, lay quivering and died, defecating. I believe the cartoon was called 'Suffering Cats'. It was seditious.

A challenging case. Today we talked.

LANE: Good morning, Hank. Feeling OK today?

HANK: Try a synthesis of that.

LANE: I'd like to try—

HANK: They're out of it. No good. (Indistinct murmur) Pricks! (Or 'bricks')

LANE: I'd like you to look at these cards and tell me what the story is on each. What they remind you of.

HANK: Listen, I'm the pope around here. I'm the mural man and I'm the muracle man . . .

LANE: What does this remind you of, Hank? (Overturned car)

HANK: It's a picture that's supposed to remind me of the next picture. It reminds me a little of a car accident. And a mural I once did, about fifteen hundred miles long. Incorporated a white line, nothing nicer.

LANE: Do you think doing murals is nice, Hank? Isn't it more fun building things up, painting, than tearing them down?

HANK: Why choose? They don't. It's all part of the same thing, the seduction of the construction. If you're looking for anarchist bombers, arrest God, eh? There's the destruction of the destruction for you!

Anyway, it's too late. You can't exactly make an omelet, can you? One of these days, 'Up against the wall, robot!' and it's good-bye Mexico. Their symbol the cockroach, the meek little bastard that inherits the earth.

I gather he's talking about building walls, painting murals on them and then tearing them down. This doubtless symbolizes his whole life, a tension between creation (art) and destruction (anarchy). A long and wasted life! It's hard to believe, but Hank was born before the great Chesterton died.

A Harsh Physic (I)

The roomful of psychologists and police officials paid little attention when the President entered. Some were gossiping, and those who noticed his scurrying figure turned away with disgusted expressions: 'That slick bastard . . . Let's talk about something else . . .'

It was different when they saw Bissell of the FBI coming straight from the door to the lectern. The admiration, envy and affection they felt for the little guy could not be expressed in ordinary terms – though perhaps Freemasons had a word for the stirring beneath the apron.

Bissell gave his report on surveillance. On the whole, random search and arrest techniques had not proved productive of info on subverts. Intensive infiltration was being tried with more success, but it took time, men and money.

'We managed to infiltrate one group of anarchist bombers in the Southwest, for example, only by an indirect method. Our man on the inside is not actually known to us – we couldn't risk direct contact. Instead he passes information to the Bureau and receives orders from it through a neutral man. We call him a "circuit-breaker", because he can break contact in case of trouble.

'Our "Listening Post" program has been very successful,' he continued. 'This means bugging public and private places where we hope dangerous subverts might meet. Originally we had planned to use computers to sort through the vast amount of tape we collected this way. The computers would search for key words like *black*, *power*, *liberation*, *revolution* and *government*, and select these portions for further study.

'But we have recruited instead a large number of personnel to do this sorting job for us. These recruits are trustworthy, keen listeners, naturally suspicious and absolutely loyal. Best of all, they work for free.'

The President raised his hand. 'Just who are these dedicated personnel?'

'I was about to explain, sir, that they are elderly people living in retirement homes. As they have little to do, listening gives them pleasure. Many are retired military men, only too glad to still be of service to their country.'

That concluded Bissell's report. Flanked by two of his enormous agents, the little man marched out of the room. The rest realized they had been holding their breaths. Now the place seemed empty, as though it had lost some great dynamic presence – some modern Wilhelm Reich.

At the Rocking R

Brad Dexter peered out of his water-cooled window at America Deserta. As always, hot and quiet. Fifty degrees out there, or so the ranch authorities said, and a laborious calculation told him that this was 'a hundred and twenty-two real degrees, Irma! Think of that!'

He propped her up so she could see the shimmering desert. 'You know, in the old days, they used to fry an egg on the sidewalk on a day like this. No, I guess they only pretended to fry it. I found out later it was a fake, in *Unvarnished Truth* magazine. I got the issue here someplace.'

Much of the small room was taken up with towering stacks of magazines. The ranch authorities hadn't liked it, but Brad had insisted on not parting with a single issue of *Unvarnished Truth*. If a man couldn't live in comfort at a retirement ranch, just where in hell could he relax? Just tell Brad that, and he would ask no more.

It wasn't much of a ranch. No horses, cattle, barns, corrals or pastures. In fact, it wasn't a ranch at all, except for being stuck out here in the blazing desert. The Rocking R Retirement Ranch consisted of thirteen great hexagonal towers called 'bunkhouses', each named after some forgotten child star. Brad and Irma resided on the twentieth story of Donald O'Connor.*

'Now where is that article?' Brad leafed through tattered, yellowed issues containing the latest on the Kennedy assassinations, 'I Killed Martin Bormann', 'Her Hubby Was a Woman', 'Eyeless Sight', 'Birth Pills Can Kill!' and 'How Oil Companies Murdered the Car That Runs on Water'. 'I know I had that danged thing someplace— What are you looking at, honey?'

There wasn't much to see outside. Everything was so still it could have been a hologram. The electric fence that marked the future location of the Wall made a diagonal across this picture, starting in the lower right corner and disappearing over a dune at the upper left. Next to it an endless sausage curl of barbed wire followed the same contour. Somewhere beyond the dune lay the work camp where they were building the Wall. Once a week, Brad had been lucky enough to see a great silver airship carrying equipment and supplies to the camp, and now he hoped Irma had spotted another. It was funny about Irma. Even though her eyes never moved, Brad could always tell when she was intent on something.

Now he saw it, a tiny figure trudging along next to the barbed wire coil, coming this way. From here, Brad couldn't make out much except the gray uniform.

'Escapee from the work camp, Irma. And there goes the danged lunch bell. Well, to heck with that – this is worth missing lunch for!' He took out his teeth for comfort.

The work camp prisoners were all political agitators, commies, anarchists and others who had tried to overthrow the government by force. Brad had got to see some of them closer up when they came to do some work on the roof of Shirley

* The other bunkhouses were Shirley Temple, Margaret O'Brien, Butch Jenkins, Baby Leroy, Bobby Driscoll, Jackie Cooper, Elizabeth Taylor, Judy Garland, Luana Patten, Mickey Rooney, Dean Stockwell and Skippy Homeier.

Temple. They had built an enormous black box up there – something to do with the security system for the Wall. Brad guessed it was radar. The prisoners had all looked well fed and contented, probably better off than a lot of people that had worked hard all their lives, like Brad.

'This should be good,' he said, breaking wind with excitement. 'That fool has been slogging along God knows how many miles in this heat, and all for nothing. They'll get him. Always do, or so they tell me. I figure they won't even bother looking for him until they've let him bake his brains a little. They know what they're doing, all right. There, what did I tell you?'

A helicopter cruiser had now come over the hill. It moved slowly along the barbed wire as though tracking the fugitive, though he was in plain sight. Looking back, he speeded up his walking movements, though his progress was still hopeless. Gradually the spray of dust raised by the rotors advanced, erasing his footprints.

As the cruiser closed in, the pedestrian threw himself down and tried to dig in like a crab. But the magic circle of blowing dust overtook and enclosed him. The helicopter paused, turning, poking its rear in the air, excited by the kill.

When it rose, the man was flopping in a net, a neat package hanging from the insect belly. Brad watched it out of sight.

'By Godfrey, Irma, wasn't that something? Our boys really know their stuff. It made me proud to be living here in the greatest country on earth. And to think that our boys are building our First Line of Defense right here where we can see it! God, it's grand, old girl!'

The second lunch bell rang, and Brad decided to eat after all. At least today he'd have something to tell Harry Boggs, instead of the other way around. Harry thought the world revolved around him and his Listening Post work. Gossip-gathering was all it really amounted to.

'Only, today I've got better gossip!' Brad slipped in his teeth and grimaced them into position, then off he went. Irma, being an inflatable, had of course no need to eat.

Captain Middlemass

That week the residents of Donald O'Connor bunkhouse were treated to an official lecture on the Wall. Captain Mallery Middlemass turned out to be all they could have hoped, a well-burnished young man, glowing with health. They all savored the depth of his chest, the breadth of his shoulders, the rich timbre of his voice. So unlike the usual visitors, either down-at-heels entertainers like 'The Amazing Lepantos' or else retired folk from other bunkhouses, people with frail lungs, uneven shoulders and thin, dry hair. The captain's hair was shiny black as patent leather, and his eyes were dark-glowing garnets.

He explained that the Wall was a population barrier. While our own population was increasing at a reasonable rate, that of Mexico was completely out of control.

'For years the slow poisons have been seeping across the border: marijuana, pornography, VD and cheap labor. They have seeped into America's nervous system, turning our kids into drug addicts, infecting their minds and bodies with filth and stealing away American jobs. Poverty and its handmaidens, crime and vice, are spreading across the nation like cancer. They have one source: Spanish America!'

He showed them the model and explained some of the Wall's special features. It would incorporate (on the Mexican side) sophisticated electronic detection equipment and weapons, capable of marking the sparrow's fall, and (on our side) part of a new highway network connecting retirement ranches with new Will Doody Funvilles.

Brad and Harry got in line to shake the captain's hand. Up close they could see that he was not so young, after all. The sagging patches of yellow skin around his eyes really were a case for *Unvarnished Truth.*

3. The Bang Gang

A Harsh Physic (II)

After Bissell, a police training expert spoke on riot control. 'The first step is knowing when and where a riot is going to start. We can often control this factor by "priming the pump", or staging a catalytic incident ourselves.'

'Just a minute!' The Great Seal looked concerned. 'Isn't that provocation? Is it legal?'

'It is, the way we do it, yes, sir. We just have one man dressed as a demonstrator "attacked", "brutally beaten" and "arrested" in sight of the mob. All simulated, of course. My department has never been against using street theater in this way – and it's legal.

'Once things are in motion, we have other choices: We can contain, control or divert a riot. Sometimes we even "de-control" it, or let it get out of hand. If a mob does enough damage, we usually find public opinion hardened against them.

'Our actual techniques are too numerous to describe – the menu of gases alone is enormous. I might mention one experiment: giving tactical police a rage-inducing drug prior to their going on duty. A related experiment is hate-suggestion TV in the duty bus. On their way to the scene of action the boys are given a dose of King Mob at his ugliest. This has produced a nine percent increase in arrests, and a whopping seventeen percent increase in nonpolice casualties! It seems worth further investigation.

'A lot of riot work is the job of the evidence and public relations squads. The evidence squad guarantees convictions for riot crimes: conspiracy to disorder, incitement to riot and unlawful assembly. One way of doing this is to issue what we call "black" publications. These are posters, leaflets and newspapers made to look like real "underground" items, but we've added to them certain incriminating articles. After all, the *real* intentions of these radicals are to bomb and shoot the ordinary, decent citizens into submission, and it's time we exposed them for what they are! Our evidence squad is headed by a man with considerable experience, the former editor of *Unvarnished Truth* magazine.

'The public relations squad helps edit film and TV tape of riots, to help the public understand what we are doing. They remove portions that might be used to smear our tactical police forces. The national networks have all been very cooperative in this effort to close the "communications gap" and keep the American public informed. It all adds up to a whale of a lot of work for us, but we like it that way. We believe that there's no such thing as a terrible riot – just bad publicity.'

Up the Sleeves

'The question is, why is it legal to be a cop?' Chug asked. The crowd, gathered to watch him and Ayn performing, were caught off balance. 'The cop is clearly employed by the criminal, to spread crime and disorder.'

'Commie!' A bottle crashed at Chug's feet.

'Another vote for law and order,' he remarked, and went right on. 'Ever see a cop eat a banana?'

Ayn and Chug usually got a crowd by doing tricks. Ayn, in pink spangled tights and with her black hair flowing free, would swallow fire. Then Chug would take over. In immaculate evening dress, he'd stride about the cleared circle, producing fans of cards and lighted cigarettes from the air. Now that they had Ras to sell pamphlets down front, it became a smoother show. The crowds were bigger, but nastier.

Someone threw another bottle. Ayn picked up a big piece of it and took a healthy bite. The crowd was so quiet that all could hear her crunching glass. After a moment Chug resumed his speech, whipping them up to such wild enthusiasm that one or two reckless citizens bought nickel pamphlets from Ras.

'Why is our corporation government so worried about Mexico?' Chug asked. 'Why are they willing to spend more money on building a wall against the Mexican poor than has been spent on the welfare of our own poor in fifty years? Could it be that mere humanity is becoming an embarrassment to our standard oil government?'

'Go back to Russia!'

'Russia is a state of mind. Why don't we all go back to a human state of mind? Why is it more illegal now to blow up an empty government office building, hurting no one, than to drop tons of bombs and burning gasoline on civilian farm families?

Is it because the first is something the people do to a government, while the second—'

The next missile was a tire iron. It spun high against the lemon Jell-O sky and down, knocking off Chug's silk hat. Grinning desperately, he produced two bouquets of feather flowers. Under cover of this misdirection, Ayn escaped to get the car. She picked up Ras first, then circled the crowd to get Chug as the rocks and bottles started reaching for him. Ras opened the door and a brickbat clipped Chug in.

'The crowd wasn't angry,' he said, mopping blood with a string of bright silk squares. 'Someone started that. Someone in back.'

'I know, I saw them,' said Ras. 'Lambs.* Four of them. I noticed when they got out of their Cadillac, with coats over their arms to hide the tire irons and bats. I tried to warn you, but they were too quick.'

'Well, it shows they care.'

Ayn, Chug and Ras

Although various people drifted in and out of the group centered on OK's Bookstore, Ayn and Chug were its constant twin nuclei. Formerly 'The Amazing Lepantos', they had fallen into revolution as a new gimmick, an addition to their repertoire. What a show-stopper, to finish with government for good! But now the gimmick had ensleeved them. Ayn ran the bookstore, which specialized in the occult and so drew those hungering for utopia.

But instead of the indigestible stone of Marxist tracts, Ayn gave them the bread of poetry. OK Press produced pamphlets calling no one brother, exhorting none to rise up or join in, making no demand to stand up and be counted. *The Garden of Regularity* was a spirited defense of cannibalism on the

* Lambs: a vigilante group borrowing rhetoric and enthusiasm from the late 'silent patriot', S. Agnew: 'They call us pigs, but we are really sacrificial lambs. We will not bandy epithets, but gladly give our lives to sweep this country clean of its plethora of pusillanimous liberals and their drug-pushing, parasitical radical associates.'

grounds of its 'natural laxative effects', while *Think Again, Mr Big Business!* was a pornographic radio play. One unaccountably popular item was a movie scenario by 'Phil Nolan', called *The U— S— of A—*.

Chug was a spare-time anarchist, as he had been a spare-time Lepanto. His real job was mechanical designer for Will Doody Enterprises. It was Chug who choreographed the antics of the robot animals that made up each Doody Funville show.

Bison and beaver were programmed to dance and sing the stories of famous Americans, all of them Unforgettable Characters. A caribou related the musical story of the invention of the telephone by 'Mr Ring-a-ding-dingy Bell' Otters caroled of Abner Doubleday's game. The pleasanter parts of the legend of John D. Rockefeller were repeated by a shy, long-lashed brontosaurus.

In the Doody world it was always Saturday afternoon in a small Midwestern town of 1900. Science was represented by Tom Edison, poetry by Ed Guest, painting by Norm Rockwell and Grandma Moses, literature by Booth Tarkington and Horatio Alger, culture by the ice cream parlor and politics by the barbershop. And all was interpreted by cuddly robots.

Currently Chug was arranging the linkages of a duck to enable it to duckspeak of Thomas Paine:

> Yup, yup! He was a firebrand
> And his brand of fire
> Was more than old King George could stand.

The song omitted mention of how Paine had died: old, lonely and so despised by the Americans whose freedom he'd labored for that they could not suffer him to sit in a stagecoach with decent folk. In spare moments at work, Chug drew sketches for impossibly elaborate singing bombs.

Ras became the third steadfast member of the group. He was an unemployed high school teacher who apparently drifted to them and stuck. Running the press, minding the store, handing out pamphlets – nothing was too much trouble for him. That's because he was, as everyone knew perfectly well, a police spy.

Ras found it hard to infiltrate them, not because they were secretive, but because they seemed to have no secrets at all. They were careless about publicity, and indeed, the group had never been given a name. Baffled by their openness, Ras kept digging. He never doubted for a moment that they had concealed a sinister purpose, like Chesterton's anarchists, under a cloak of jolly anarchy.

'Where do we keep the bombs?' he would ask.

'Up here,' Ayn would say, tapping her head with solemn significance. 'Truth be our dynamite.'

'And Justice our permanganate,' Chug would add. 'And our blasting caps be Freedom, Honor and—'

'No, really. The real bombs.'

They hated to disappoint him. 'You'll know soon enough, Ras. It's just that we hate to tell you too soon, in case you fell into the hands of the police or anything.'

Then Chug and Ayn would go off somewhere and laugh, while Ras went to report. It never occurred to them to 'deal with' him in any way, or even to withdraw their friendship. He was, after all, a needed romantic figure, an Informer. Without him the group would have been dull indeed.

The Circuit Breaker

Ras was supposed to be giving old Mr Eric von Jones tuition in mathematics. Shortly after each lesson, Mr von Jones would take a piano lesson from an FBI agent. In this way Ras and the agent communicated without knowing each other's name or face.

'Have you completed the problems I assigned?'

Somehow asking Mr von Jones the simplest question set off in him an elaborate cycle of clockwork twitches and tics: hand to mouth, roll of eye, lift of brow and shrug of shoulder. The cycle took a full minute to complete.

'Yes . . . here.' The old man slid across the dining table a dozen sheets of carefully written equations. On the last page were Ras's orders.

'Fine. Now here's your corrected work from last time.' Ras slid back to him a report on the OK's Bookstore group. 'Now, shall we go over some trigonometric ratios?'

The twitches unwound once more. 'Yes . . . I'd like that.' Squaring his notebook with the corners of the table, he selected one of a dozen pencils all sharpened to the same length and headed the page 'Notes'.

'You don't need to really take notes,' Ras whispered.

'I'm very . . . interested in ratios.'

Ras looked at him: a corpse at attention. No doubt Mr von Jones made the FBI man teach him scales too. That parsnip-colored face seemed to glow only at the prospect of some tiresome duty. Probably he would go on from one chore to another, carrying himself through routine motions for a few more years, until at last he was called to the great treadmill in the sky.

Dr Lane's Secret Journal (II)

I can't understand how Hank knew they were going to build a wall along the border. One with a 'white line . . . fifteen hundred miles long', which is a highway! It all seemed just babbling at the time, but now even the 'good-bye Mexico' makes sense. I have also just learned that a Will Doody Funville is to be built somewhere in the area, against the wall. No doubt 'Up against the wall, robot!' refers to Doody's robot animals!

This seems to be a genuine case of clairvoyance. There is just no other rational explanation!

Harry Boggs on Life

Harry gave an after-dinner lecture on the subject 'Is There Life on Other Planets?' to a dozen other residents of Donald O'Connor bunkhouse. He concluded that there certainly was, and that it was of the utmost importance to get in contact with the Uranians.

'That's the real reason they're building this wall,' he said. 'With powerful telescopes, the Uranians will be able to see it.'

Another important means of communication could be telepathy, he went on, but most of us had our telepathic equipment damaged by a lack of vital sea kelp in our diet. When he'd finished, four or five white heads in the audience nodded, as if in agreement. Brad Dexter's was among them; Harry had seen bundles of *Unvarnished Truth* on a cart, bound for the incinerator. And draped over the top bundle, what looked like a deflated rubber dolly . . .

No time for such thoughts now, of course. Time for Harry's important government work. Red-faced and breathless with vision, he hurried to his room and tuned in on Listening Post.

'Number 764882. Number 764882,' said an announcer slowly, so he could copy it down. Two women's voices came on the air.

'. . . a slipped disk. But all in all, it wasn't bad.'

'Haven't they got any forjias? No? OK, bring me the roast sud. What did you say his name was?'

Harry was happier talking about his important government work than actually doing it, but he soldiered along. The FBI expected him to listen to an hour a day of this:

'Impinging upon my career. The great chain of buying, that's what it is. Impinging and impugning . . . impugn sort . . . Sri Mantovani . . . Einstein and people like Einstein said that the world was flat . . . reliance . . . bargain jay or meep . . .'

Harry vowed that he would never again say anything dull or unimportant in a public place.

MEMO: From the desk of A. Lincoln

I generally find that a man slow to get a joke is slow to win a battle. That is why I like to see my generals piss-eyed with laughter at all times. General Ned Allison tells me he knows of three soldiers, who had been imbibing, and were sent to a certain address in Gettysburg – but I expect that this is just one of Ned's 'leg-pullers'. Hope you and Martha are well. I and the missus are tolerable.

The Séance

Chug and Ayn had wanted to go, so much so that Ras suspected a secret meeting. Perhaps this 'séance' was really the place where they received their orders, from the Central Council of

Anarchists. He'd volunteered to go with them, and they'd insisted he go in their place. There was his dilemma: Were they getting him out of the way while they went elsewhere, or were they trying to bluff him out of the séance?

He went, still vaguely expecting the Central Council, men in beards and dark glasses, calling themselves Breakfast, Coffee Break, Lunch, Tea, Dinner, Supper and Midnight Snack . . .

The medium was an anemic old lady with knotty flesh hanging from her arms, Mrs Ross. The others were Hank James (an old man with mad eyes), Dr Lane (looked like a young optician), Mrs Paris (a plump old lady with an asthmatic Pekingese and a hat of similar material) and Steiner, a young man with erupting skin.

As soon as the lights went out, Ras felt another presence, an enormous fat man who almost filled the room. In the deep blind blackness it was terrifying, for Ras dared not move for fear of touching the fat man.

The medium did not speak. After a moment, Ras said, 'I thought it wasn't supposed to work with a skeptic in the room.'

A deep, fat voice came back at once: 'Don't be an ass. That's what these fraud mediums tell you, but don't listen to them. Actually it *only* works when there is *at least one* skeptic in the room.'

'Who are you?'

'Some call me God, Allah, Jaweh, the All, the Other, the Great Imponderable, Bingo, Mammon, the Light, names like that. Call me what you like, but call me in time for dinner.'

Ras shuddered at the use of that particular noun. 'Are you the chief of the anarchists, then?'

'Why must there be a chief? Maybe we all walk shoulder to shoulder, shank to shank. No leaders.'

'Not your kind. You need kings to kill, at least. And presidents and bishops and gods – all targets for your bombs.'

'Go on. I find it fascinating the way reactionaries assume all the bombs and guns are turned against them. Who raises the armies, builds the rockets, buys the bombs, draws the border and declares war, if not your kings and presidents?'

'I should warn you,' Ras said through gritted teeth, 'I am an agent of the FBI.' The time for caution was past.

'That is obvious, and needs no warning. But you'd better warn me if you feel a change of heart coming on.'

'No danger of that, my fat friend!'

'Ah! But if you say that, you are on the very brink of conversion to anarchy!'

'But you are the forces of anarchy. You are they who hate and fear the light, they who hate order because it is orderly, life because it is alive.'

'Am I?'

Suddenly it was all wrong. Ras felt as if he had betrayed himself, to himself. *He* was the anarchist, and this voice the spirit of Law and Order, of J. Edgar Hoover, of—

'Damn you!' he shrieked. 'Damn you, Chesterton!'

'Chesterton?' said the voice as the lights came up. 'But my dear chap, Chesterton is simply other people.'

Mrs Ross opened her eyes and beamed. 'My, how successful we have been!' she said. 'Two strong emanations! I think I liked the one called Chesterton best, though the late FBI agent was nice too.'

Dr Lane's Secret Journal (III)

Dr Veck has refused to accept my parapsychological explanation of Hank's predictions. He's refused to even discuss them. But I tried Hank out at a séance and also with ESP cards, with interesting results. At the séance I actually spoke with the spirit of Chesterton, and heard him curse himself! This may not be Hank's influence, of course. Still, there are the ESP scores. His psychosis seems to have brought him near to some crack in the fabric of futurity so that his inner eye *sees through*! If Dr Veck continues trying to suppress this discovery of national importance, I may have to unleash Hank's terrible power upon him.

Hank's terrible power is that he knows the future – which means the future is in some way here already! We need only ask him what to do, and receive the awful impress of his ESPing reply.

PS. I find my concentration on receiving ESP messages is much keener when I restrict my diet to brown foods – brown eggs, bread, sugar and rice – and to iron-rich foods such as molasses. Perhaps the iron sets up induction currents. But I must retain control. Hysteresis is the path to hysteria.

Ratio

'I haven't got any "corrected problems" for you this time. In fact I feel like giving all this up. Why don't you just tell your piano teacher that I can't find out any more about their bombs. About anything. And I'm not sure I care.'

'I . . . see. Well, then, how about the lesson?'

'The lesson?'

'I've already learned some of it.' To Ras's horror, the old man closed his eyes and began reciting from memory the tables of sines and cosines.

Maybe I am an anarchist. *The* anarchist. But is this law and order? Sitting here listening to a mad old man?

At $4^{\circ}\ 15'$, Ras lurched from the table.

'I . . . haven't finished.'

'I know, excuse me, I feel a little sick.' He stumbled into the dark hallway and snatched at a doorknob at random.

'No, wait! Don't open that!'

Ras crashed into a closet full of glass gallon jugs. As he recoiled, one jug tipped and fell, splattering its contents. The smell of stale piss rose about him. 'My God!'

'I'm sorry. I'm . . . very retentive, you see.'

When Ras had slammed out of the house, Mr von Jones shrugged, cleared his throat, curled his right foot around a table leg, lifted an eyebrow, coughed. A terrible scene. A terrible young man. Damage had been done and repairs were needed. Mr von Jones counted to ten thousand, to the metronome.

Resist, A Plot Is Brought Home; The Tour

Ras cornered Chug in a café. 'Listen, I have a—' He meant 'confession to make', but finished 'plan'. His voice shook, and his eyes reflected the peculiar disagreeable yellow of the Formica tables. 'We'll blow up the White House and kill the President.'

Keeping his face straight, Chug nodded. 'OK. I've got an idea for the bomb to do it with.' On the yellow Formica he sketched his design for an enormous steam-driven duck that could sing 'Taking a Chance on Love' while delivering an explosive egg.

Harry Boggs could hardly believe his good luck. But by jingo, there was no doubt about it. This 'Ras' and his pal 'Chug' were plotting assassination. This was the real thing!

Countdown

The piano teacher had brought along a piano tuner. 'Listen, Mr von Jones, we're making the raid today. We have to know the name of our contact man on the inside. I mean, is he still working for us? We haven't had a report for weeks.'

'I . . . a report?'

The two men leaned over him. 'Mr von Jones? Are you all right?'

'Look at this, Don. Pupils are different sizes. This guy's had a stroke.'

'I'm . . . fine, really. And I know the young man you mean. But his name just . . . I didn't retain it.'

The raid proceeded. The FBI succeeded in arresting all members of the gang except the one called 'Ras', who they suspected was the ringleader. The rest were interrogated and packed off to Fort Nixon for retraining as good citizens.

My Struggle

Late that night, the President worked at his memoirs in the small office attached to his bedroom.

. . . and all of the Negroes wanted to shake my hand!! Combined with the rest of the day's defeats, the pressures of responsibility for this heaviest office in the land, it was almost enough to shake my faith in my own destiny. But not quite.

I had much to be weary about. Iowa, Kansas and Nebraska

were virtually a dustbowl. South Africa and its satellite nations were getting tough about Tanzania. The War still dragged on. The steel and rail strikes still dragged on. The cities – better not spoken of. Yet I had time in the midst of the storm to share a quiet joke with General Hare. I asked if he knew what kind of boat would be a slow boat to China? The answer was, a gravy boat!

The Great Seal enjoyed his joke all over again. It was the only one he'd ever made, unless you counted the Great Wall of Mexico.

The Reagan Room

'What I want to know,' said one of the Roosevelts to another as they went off duty, 'is what he does in the Reagan Room? I've seen trays of food go in there, and a doctor.'

The other smiled the famous Roosevelt smile. 'I thought you knew. He keeps a wounded soldier in there. Some say he just sits and chats with him, gives him encouragement. But others say it's very odd that he particularly asked for a soldier with a belly wound.'

'Just a minute!' The first FDR scowled. 'That's the President you're talking about, mister. Watch yourself!'

'Now calm down. Listen, even the President might do something he's not very proud of now and then, right? I mean, he's only phocine, for Christ's sake. Try to see this thing in the greater perspective of his brilliant career.'

'OK, OK. I just said watch it, that's all.'

4. The Cockroach

Dr Lane's Secret Journal (IV)

Hank has tapped out his ESP message in no uncertain terms. I see that Dr Veck is an obstacle to science. My task is clear, for Hank has sent me a picture of Dr Veck lying in a pool of blood. It must be done. I am but the instrument of fate, or of G. K. Chesterton. Perhaps they are one and the same. O my restless, questioning soul, thirsting for truth!

Later. I did it. I killed Veck in the middle of his work on a very interesting paper on socialism and epilepsy. Hank took the news calmly, considering that he is now off drugs.

'We're all of us doomed anyway,' he said.

'Doomed?'

'The Wall. The Wall was my idea in the first place.'

'You influenced future ev—'

'I influenced my nephew. A long time ago I told my nephew an idea of mine for a Great Wall of Mexico. It was to be a giant decorated sculpture. My nephew much later became a special "creative" adviser to the President. Obviously he has put my idea into effect. Young Bill Filcup was always very enterprising.'

'But the doom?'

'Well, you and I, and this hospital-prison, and a lot of other people and places, are the decoration.'

I said I didn't understand. He laughed.

'We just haven't been applied yet,' he said.

The meaning of all this escapes me. It may be clear one day. From my window I can see the Wall, and the magnificent sunset. I

Harry

Harry thought he smelled something burning.

The U— *S— of A—*

A movie scenario by 'Phil Nolan'

Scene I. A peak in Darien. Cortez stands gazing upon the Pacific, which, it is clear from the way his men exchange glances, he has just named. He is silent.

Scene II Rapidly turning calendar pages: November 28, 29, Brumaire, 1666, Aries, November 30, 31, Ventose, 6379, 125, Thursday, 5427, New Moon.

Scene III. The Delaware River. Washington approaches, throws silver dollar across.

Scene IV. Old Glory flutters in breeze. Offscreen voices hum 'God Save the King'.

Scene V. Japanese diplomats walking out of League of Nations. Offscreen lugubrious voice: 'The treacherous Japanese insisted they were a peace-loving people, and we believed them. Then – the stab in the back that brought Mr and Mrs America to their senses. On December 7, 1941 – (cut to atomic bomb explosion) – *Pearl Harbor!*'

Scene VI. Statue of Liberty, holding up a sword. Same voice: 'At last, just as Britain has its *Neptunia* ruling the waves, just as France has its "La belle dame sans merci", now America has Mrs Liberty, welcoming the storm-tossed aliens.' (Karl Rossman passes.) 'Welcome! Welcome to the melting pot!'

Scene VII. (Animation) Caldron marked MELTING POT. Ladle pours in liquefied 'masses'. Caldron slowly sags and melts.

A Special Message from the President

The President's black-and-white image appeared on the television screen surrounded by a black condolence border. He seemed almost too humble to have a clear image. Instead the fuzzy, bleached patches of his face, oddly patterned by liver spots and furrows, gave him the look of a soiled etching.

'My countrymen, it is a grave announcement that I must make to you this evening. What I am about to say is a block of sadness and grief in the neighborhood of my heart, as I am sure it will be in yours.

'Tonight several nuclear explosions occurred at different places along the population barrier between the United States and Mexico. These explosions, let me make this perfectly clear, were accidental. No one is to blame. No one could have avoided them. Certain technical failures in our security system set off a chain of events – and Nature took its course.

'Still, there's no denying that many thousands, millions, rather, of people have been killed. Since these bombs were located on top of high-rise retirement ranches and on top of mental hospitals, they have killed many unfortunate persons, and that is to be regretted. It is also regrettable that a lethal zone has been created along our border.'

The black border vanished. Jubilant music swelled behind his voice as our leader intoned: 'On the positive side, very few of our troops in the area were injured. The Army reports only a dozen casualties. Some of Will Doody's Funville projects have been destroyed, but I am going to ask Congress to compensate Mr Doody for this terrible loss. As for the Wall itself, it has been badly burned and cratered in spots. Luckily it protects our border yet with a barrier of radiation. For the present, we are vigilant, but safe. And for the future?'

Suddenly the air about the gray President was filled with tiny, bright-colored fingers; animated elves, fairies, butterflies and bluebirds, tiny pink bats in spangled hose, flying chipmunks and dancing dragonflies. Smiling, he too burst into color. 'The future is ours, my countrymen! We will rebuild our Wall taller and stronger and safer than ever, so secure that it will last a thousand years! Come! Help me make this country strong!' He extended an arm upon which doves and butterflies were alighting already. And as the chorus sang '... from sea to shining sea', twittering bluebirds modestly covered the scene with a Star-Spangled Curtain.

Epilogue

Ras turned up again in Red Square, conspicuous in a black cape and a tall silk hat. The cane in his hand was a sword cane, naturally, and the whiskers hooked over his ears on spectacle bows. A tourist gaped for a moment, as Ras harangued a crowd of pigeons.

When he'd finished, he produced a round black bomb, lit it and tossed it into the crowd. Its small pop was enough to attract the notice of two yawning policemen, who came over to examine the three dead pigeons.

As, still stifling yawns, they escorted him away, Ras shouted slogans into the faces of other tourists. Probably they knew no English, for they stared sullenly, all but one man, who sought an explanation in his guidebook.

Afterword

When I showed this collection of stories to a friend of mine, Ms Cassandra Knye, she began questioning me closely about my dreams.

'Burning seems to be one of your obsessions,' she said. 'A burning giraffe, a burnt face (in two stories), and even a parched adjutant.'

I said I didn't understand what she was driving at, so she sat down to write (and doodle) the following interpretation:

In dreams we entertain recurring images, strung together sometimes in surprising ways. Since these stories purport to be surrealistic, it is valid to examine them as strings of dream-images. The conscious mind of Mr Sladek may try to disguise these images by elaborate transformations, but the dream-content shows through. *Burning* for example occurs throughout the collection: The first story mentions burning giraffes, and the last ends with an explosion. Another (flaming) explosion ends *Secret of the Old Custard*, while other stories (*The Face, The Master Plan* and *The Locked Room*) involve burning or parching.

The Great Wall of Mexico is an interesting disguise of the Great Wall of China (china is of course *fired* clay): The Emperor who built the Great Wall, Shih Huang Ti, 'likewise ordered all books antedating him to be *burned*'. This is according to Jorge Luis Borges, who is mentioned casually in another story, *Undecember.*

But there are other, more visible connections. If we look at the *Elephant with Wooden Leg,*

his back is an arched, load-bearing bridge, as in *The Design*:

With the legs, head and tail restored, the elephant-bridge becomes the tortoise of Aeschylus (in *Undecember*):

With the trunk and a wheel added, the elephant-bridge becomes a hay-wagon, the dominant symbol of dead weight creaking through *Scenes from Rural Life* as though it had lost a tyre:

But the hay-wagon easily transforms to the armored car (in *Secret of the Old Custard*) which is called a Welcome Wagon (note the two W's):

The elephant's wooden leg might equally be a torch for the Statue of Liberty. In *The Great Wall*, Ms Liberty has lost her torch, and may have handed it to one of the mob in *The Face*:

The elephant can roll up his trunk, which then equals a snake biting its own tail (as in *The Face*) or a tyre. The tyre is the centrepiece of a picnic in *Heavens Below*:

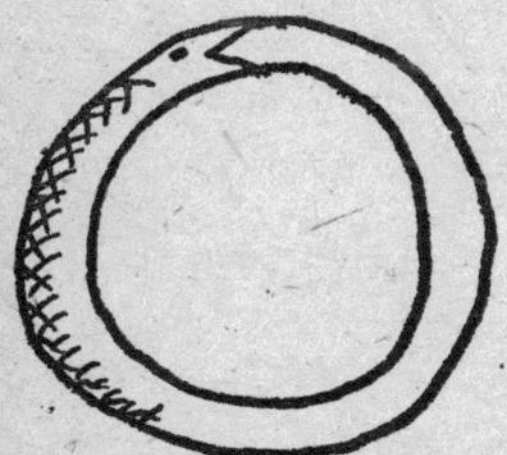

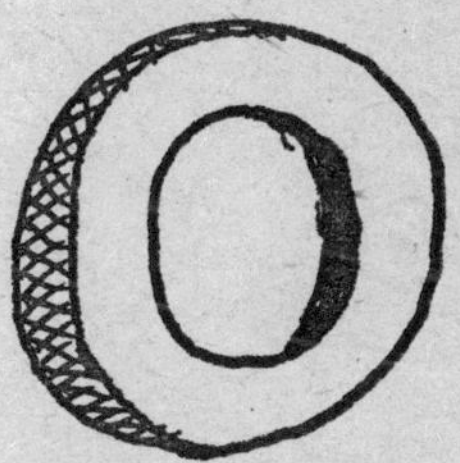

But a tyre implies a wheel, so we next look for that image. It is on the hay-wagon and the Welcome Wagon, but it turns up elsewhere: The wooden leg again may serve as a wheel and axle:

Turned on its side, the wheel and axle becomes a cake with candle (such as the cake in *A Game of Jump*):

The cake with its candle displaced to one side becomes a kind of clumsy boot (e.g., a *Space Shoe*):

The shadow of the cake with candle resembles the bomb in *Great Wall*:

But this bomb requires only a minimal change to become the ball-and-chain of *Flatland* and *The Commentaries* and *Hammer of Evil*:

The cannonball-and-chain calls to mind the Human Cannonball (*The Locked Room*) of the circus (elephants again!). His cannon is made of the wheel, the wooden leg, and the head of an elephant:

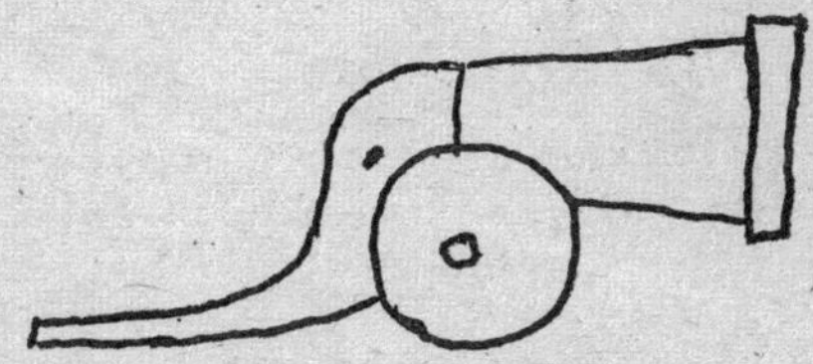

These same transformations may be performed to include the remaining stories.

Cassandra Knye

I feel that Ms Knye has missed the point, somehow.

JTS